THE OREGON TRAIL

~ Pathway to the West ~

By

Tecla Emerson

OutLook Press
210 Legion Ave. #6805
Annapolis, MD 21401
TeclaM@aol.com

Cover Design by
Katharine Sodergreen
Sodergreen@aol.com

Interior layout by Robert Henry
http://righthandpublishing.com

Dedicated to Juliet

~ may your curiosity never end ~

Oregon Country
Io
Unorganized Territory
Mexico
Mexico/ Texas

United States
1845

INTRODUCTION

The east coast of America was becoming over-crowded. Tales were being told of wide-open spaces to the west where one would find ideal weather conditions and endless farmland. Families in search of more land and a new and better life set out for the unexplored and unknown territory. They traveled in wagon trains over the rough and not well-organized trails.

To arrive in this mystical land, these daring and brave pioneers would have to traverse more than half a continent. Determined, families hitched up their wagons and set off for the months-long trek into the unknown.

There were obstacles such as fire, flood, accidents, the possibility of Indian attacks and under the less than ideal conditions, disease was all too common.

It was a costly trip. The pioneers had to sell their homes and land to outfit a wagon with food, clothing and tools. It was a treacherous and dangerous journey into unexplored territory. It was a time filled with mystery and unknowns, as there were few first-hand accounts of what they were heading into. It was 1845.

They set out with family and all their worldly goods and headed for a new life. It was a long and arduous trip and one that often was disastrous.

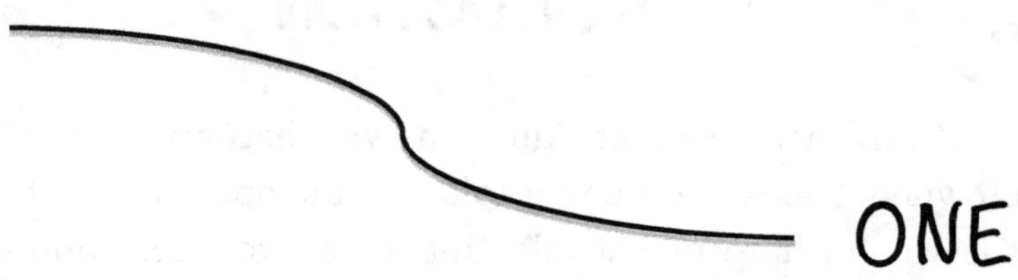

ONE

"Hannah." Why had she disappeared again? The wagons were lined up, and ready to move. The smell of new wood and canvas was thick in the air. The men fidgeted with the reins, uncomfortable with making small talk, ready to get on the trail.

Where was she?

"Hannah!" Isabelle called. "Maddie, how could you let her disappear like that?"

"Well she's not going to answer you," I said. "I'll go and find her." I hadn't meant for that to sound quite so snippy. She was my stepmother after all and I'm sure meant well. I leapt down from the wagon's high seat. Where could she be hiding now and how could a five-year-old disappear so quickly? Ever since the incident more than a year ago, Hannah had taken to hiding whenever there was a crowd of people. Either that or curling up in someone's lap, usually mine.

I was her big sister. She liked to pull an apron over her face; she thought she would disappear that way.

"Hannah, come out," This was not how I wanted to spend my last day in Virginia. If we had to go I wanted to go. Stop dilly-dallying wherever you are Hannah - but I didn't say that out loud.

Sadie came up beside me, her market basket tucked under her arm, "She gone again?" she asked.

I nodded, "Well jus' means we can be together some more." We grinned at each other, we'd been best friends practically since the day we were born. We were so different but so much the same. We were born the same month; not the same day but the same year. Growing up we'd spent summers swimming in the creek every free minute we could find and then in the fall we'd meet down by the stables and feed the horses apples. In the winter we'd slide on the ice until Sadie's mother would come and shoo us home, snapping at us that there were chores to do and we'd best get busy.

Sadie had coal black, tightly curled hair and her skin was mocha colored. I had hair that looked like it was trying to be blonde and blue eyes that my father said were about the same color as the wild Virginia bluebells.

"I wish you were coming Sadie."

"You only said that three hundred times already," she answered. "If your pa hadn't set us free, I surely would've. Guess I would've had to," she said with a smile. "Momma's not letting me out of her sight now, not since we got our manumission papers."

"I know, but think of all the fun we could have."

"But now we's free and Momma wants to settle here. Think she's 'fraid to go anywhere else."

"And ha! There she be," said Sadie pointing to the General Store. We could just see the hem of Hannah's gingham dress peeking out from behind the pickle barrel.

"Hannah..." I began, harsh words ready to erupt. I looked down at the mute child her head hanging low, her lower lip trembling. She was clutching that raggedy doll of hers to her chest. "Alright, I know, you don't want to go. But you have to." I held out my hand and let her slip hers into mine. It was small and warm.

"Wonder why she don't want to go?" Sadie mused. "Sounds like high adventure to me. Maybe she could stay here with my Momma and I'll go with you."

"I'd like that a lot. Oh gosh, I didn't mean that Hannah. I wouldn't leave you here." I looked down at the big blue eyes. They were staring at me from under the bonnet with the ties that weren't going to stay tied. I squeezed her hand. "Yes, I'd miss you."

"'S'ppose she'll ever speak again?" Sadie asked.

"Don't know. Teacher said whenever she saw someone like that, they never spoke again. Once a mute, always a mute."

"It's been more'n a year hasn't it?" she asked, her dark eyes stared into me as if there were more to the story.

"Seems like it," I answered. We were walking too fast. Hannah was struggling to keep up with us.

"Maddie, where have you been?" Isabelle asked. She leaned down to help Hannah up on the wagon. She had that cross look, her brows drawn together in a thin line, "And Sadie, won't your mother be looking for you?"

"Yes Ma'am," she answered. She didn't meet Isabelle's eyes. Sadie and I looked at each other out of the corner of our eyes trying not to smile.

"Maddie, you can either walk along by the side or come up here on the seat."

Before I could answer, I heard my uncle yell. "All up." The crack of his whip sang through the air.

Sadie and I looked at each other once again. She'd been my best friend, my only friend for so long, and now I might never see her again.

"Maddie come along now," Isabelle's tone was disapproving. "Sadie needs to get home."

"Goodbye," said Sadie, she grabbed my hand, "my friend…"

I didn't want to be caught crying but the tears welled up. I turned in a whirl, my dress catching around my ankles, nearly tripping me. I kept my head down as I rushed to catch up with the wagon. Neighbors and friends were lining the road as one after another wished us well, "Good luck," or "Godspeed," or "Write to us when you get there." "We'll miss you."

And then we were alone. There was only the sound of the animal hooves plodding along. I wanted to turn back for just one last look but was afraid I'd run back. I concentrated hard – watch where you're stepping. Concentrate. It kept the tears from falling. The ground was soft underfoot. The frost had left a while ago. The morning sun felt warm and the creak of the wagon wheels was somehow comforting.

The trip had been months in the planning. How had it crept up so fast? I wasn't ready. I wanted to go back to the big house; I wanted to go back to my own room, to the things I'd left behind. Someone else was living in my room now, but I didn't want to think about it.

All week we'd been saying goodbye, but it still didn't make it easier. We said our farewells to families I'd known all my life. And then last night, by myself, I had once more gone to the place with the white picket fence that held the gray monuments to things of the past. There were only ten headstones. Two of them still not covered by the green moss that crept up in the night, covering old granite.

It had been dusk; I had picked a bunch of the wild Virginia bluebells that grew so freely in the meadow. I put a few sprigs on each of the two graves. My feet stayed rooted to the spot; how could we leave this place, my home for all of my 15 years. Would anyone tend to the two graves? Why did we have to go?

There was really only one live blood relative who we were leaving. That was the hardest. It was Grandmom. She was too old to travel. Too old to be part of what they were calling the new adventure. Somehow, when I hugged her for what must have been the hundredth time, I knew it was our last goodbye. I knew I'd never see her again. She was the mother of the three boys, now men; my father Stewart, who was already out west and my two uncles, the twins Bert and David. They were traveling with us.

Old as they were, the twin uncles saying goodbye to Grams had been the hardest goodbye of all. Grams sat and just let the tears run down her cheeks not even dabbing at them with her ever-present handkerchief. They dribbled off the folds of skin wrinkled with age and caring. Her cloudy blue eyes just stared as the tears brimmed over. The twins were Grams favorites; nobody seemed to mind, they weren't around all that much; they just drifted in and out of her life whenever they were able to get back home. Neither had ever married although there were rumors of squaws.

Every now and again, they'd reappear after their fur trapping expeditions. They always stayed with Grams. She missed them sorely when they weren't nearby. They too had decided the West was calling out to them and it sounded as though they were ready to stop their wanderlust and settle down. Both Bert and David had grey streaks through their beards and laugh wrinkles at the corners of their eyes. Time's gonna catch up to you my father had told them. You ever gonna settle down, best do it soon.

"Maddie," said Jacob. "What's up?" His words cut into my memories, bringing me back to the moment. He flicked the reins on the backs of the oxen keeping the supply wagon moving and keeping up with the train's pace.

"Go away Jacob, leave me be." I tried to wave him off; he could be an awful annoyance at times.

"Go away yourself," he said.

"Why are you such a know-it-all?" I asked as I turned around to look up at him. He was 14 and sat there proud as a peacock, hair as usual, hanging in his eyes, hat pulled low and a half smile on his face. I saw him just as my younger brother, but he had a man's job driving the cumbersome wagon and he was proud of it.

"Not a know-it-all, just asked you a simple question," he said. "No call to be so huffy."

I ignored him. It was going to be a long five months with just the six other families. But, if luck was with us once we made it to Independence, we would be able to connect with more wagons bound for Oregon Country. That was all the way in Missouri, a long way away.

My feet were tired already; I hated the new

boots that Isabelle made me wear. I wanted to go barefoot but she used that tone. So I thought for the first day out maybe I'd listen if only to keep the peace. I was debating whether it would be worth climbing up on the wagon seat to sit next to her and to Hannah. And, as if she read my thoughts, Isabelle leaned down and asked if I wanted to ride.

"Alright," I thought that might be the lesser of the two major annoyances in my life, my brother Jacob and my stepmother Isabelle. Maybe if I rode up with her she'd stop hassling me. Hoisting myself up the side, I was careful to avoid the turning wagon wheel. I didn't want to end up like Patty Irving. Heard tell that she still doesn't walk right.

Isabelle and Hannah made room for me.

"Don't know why she ran off like that," my stepmother said, her eyes looking down at the child.

"But she always does," I said, talking as though Hannah wasn't even there. "She just doesn't like a bunch of people all around, it makes her nervous. Doesn't it," I asked pulling at one of Hannah's braids. She smiled her five-year-old smile at me and for all the world looked as normal as any young girl. She looks like Mother I thought, or what I remember of her. Her reddish blonde hair was wispy around her face and her blue eyes stared up at me adoringly.

"It's OK Hannah, no one here will hurt you." At this Hannah turned and buried her face in Isabelle's apron. I ignored it; it was hard to tell just what would set her off.

"Well," said Isabelle, "This is the beginning of the great adventure. Wish your father was here." She coughed; her shoulders shook as she tried to muffle it in her handkerchief.

So do I, so do I, I said to myself. I wasn't going to let Isabelle know just how concerned I was without Father to lead the way.

"Good thing your two uncles are here to help, we couldn't have done this alone." As she spoke Uncle David rode up on his chestnut gelding, tipping his hat and greeting my stepmother. "Isabelle, how goes it?"

"We seem to be doing well so far," she answered, muffling a final cough in her handkerchief.

"We'll be pulling up for lunch in three, four hours," he said. "That'll be our first stop. Don't plan to stay long, too far to go to be dilly-dallying. What say you to that Miss Maddie?"

"Just fine," I answered. I blushed, I didn't

mean to.

"Fine dress you're wearing," he said. I always blushed with Uncle David. For as long as I can remember, he always paid me special attention and he flirted with me. He actually sounded like he meant it when he said something nice. No one else had ever said much nice to me except Sadie — but then Sadie liked everything so it was hard to tell.

"Your Uncle Bert's doing just fine so far as our leader, seems to know where we're going." He chuckled, "Course we're hardly out of the neighborhood yet."

"Do you think it's really going to be five months?" I asked. Guess it came out kind of whiny, which I really didn't mean.

"Well now, we'll know better once we're past the mountains and stopped in Independence. If all goes well, it shouldn't be more'n a couple of months past that." Then added "Maybe more," but it was almost a whisper. As he spoke his long fingers scratched at something in his graying beard. "Just think though, by the time we all get out there, maybe it'll be part of these United States." He laughed. "Hard to know."

"Is that going to be a problem," asked Isabelle.

"I doubt it," he answered. "There's a good amount who've already headed out there and haven't really heard of any troubles. 'Sides," he said, "It should be ours before much longer. They're working on it" He took off his hat and wiped at the sweat collecting on his brow. "Polk wants expansion," he added as an afterthought.

Well at least I knew who President Polk was, but I wasn't so sure about expansion. I was happy in Virginia. And if it was true that the Oregon Country was British, why exactly were we heading out there? Sounded like trouble to me.

But Uncle had already changed the subject. "We're certainly leaving early enough, earlier than we actually had to, but it gives us a good head start. Long as we don't hit any late spring snows we'll go 'long just fine. Pretty exciting now isn't it Hannah Belle?" he asked, directing his question to the one blue eye peeking out at him from under Isabelle's apron. His eyes were crinkled up in a face with a near permanent smile. "Sorry for ye' Isabelle, that my brother didn't make it back to accompany us."

"It's quite alright," she responded. "He's to join us in Missouri. He wanted to get settled out there before we all joined him. He's put his trust in you and Bert to transport us. I'm not worried.

I'm sure all will go well." Her clipped New England accent gave an edge to her voice.

"Certainly hope so," he responded and for just a moment, I thought his eyes darkened, but when I looked again it was gone.

"Need to get up forward, see if the Barnes' are doing alright with that new ox of theirs. Too bad they didn't have time to get acquainted 'fore they hooked him up."

"I'm sure they'll be fine," said Isabelle. "Ben Barnes knows animals as well as anyone. He has helped us a few times with our stock."

"Nevertheless, I'll be on my way." He tipped his hat, his long hair getting caught up on the brim.

"We shall see you for lunch then," called Isabelle as he trotted ahead.

"Too bad their ox died," I said, "and just before we left too. Looked to me like he'd gotten into some poison or something the way he was all swoll up."

"Swollen up," said Isabelle.

"That's what I meant." I didn't mean to but I scowled.

"And what of the Barnes children?" asked Isabelle setting off a new wave of coughing. She ignored it and went on "They all seem to be doing well on this venture."

"They're all too young to even know what they're about," I said. "The oldest is only four, and it doesn't appear he knows what's happening. Too bad he's not a girl he would've been a nice friend for Hannah." I patted Hannah's sleeping head. It hadn't taken much to lull the young child into drowsiness with the sway of the wagon.

"Why do you suppose she doesn't speak?" asked my stepmother for the hundredth time, more as a musing aloud than a real question.

"She was so frightened. Maybe she saw who kilt Randy and it scared the words right out of her."

"Killed not kilt." She said, slipping in her correction before continuing. Must she always do that? Do I always need correcting? But she continued without missing a beat, "That was well over a year ago, she was talking so well back then."

The conversation was going nowhere; the niceness in me was already wearing thin. Talking about Randy wasn't my favorite topic. Everyone seemed to have an opinion on what happened to him. Who shot him and why. I decided it would be more comfortable walking than listening to Isabelle's prattle.

"Well, and where are you going?" she asked as I leapt down.

"I need to walk awhile, I'm getting cramped up there," I answered. I could hear Isabelle's dry hacking cough as the wagon rolled past. If I walk slowly, they'll get some distance ahead of me and maybe I could walk next to some other wagon for a while.

TWO

We hadn't been on the trail that many days. The Cumberland Gap was already behind us. It was just as it said - a gap. A gap that cut through the mountains. The Appalachians. As we crested one of the hills Uncle Bert said "Stand still." Which I did.

Then he said, "You're now standing in Tennessee, Kentucky and Virginia all at the same time." Well, I'd never done that before. Hannah heard him and although she didn't know that much about geography, she smiled and dashed over to stand next to me.

I wasn't really sure if he was just fooling with us but I knew all those states somehow came together near the Gap. I knew that Daniel Boone had been the one opening it up so's travelers could get to the west, or so they said. Course we all knew it was really just an old Indian trail but it wasn't my place to argue.

We hadn't traveled that far and already it was getting tiresome. Other than one of the Uncles riding up to joke with us now and again, I had walked mostly alone. I needed to find some way to pass the time. No sooner had that thought drifted away then there was the Applegate wagon. I didn't know them that well but they seemed to enjoy most everything and could be relied on to say something cheery, no matter how dismal circumstances were. And sure enough, Mrs. Applegate called down to me.

"Now isn't that just a pretty bonnet that you've picked to be traveling with today." I smiled up at her, "And I know for sure one young lady who isn't happy wearing a bonnet and just look how pretty it is." She didn't comment directly that I wasn't wearing my bonnet but merely had it tied around my neck letting it fall down my back. Mrs. Applegate was like that. Never criticizing. She could point things out but she didn't make you mad saying it.

I always enjoyed being around both of the Applegates, they seemed to laugh a lot. I never was real sure what exactly had happened with their children. The two boys Alfred and Jerome were about as lazy as any ten and eleven-year-old boys could be.

Mrs. Applegate excused herself as she spoke back into the wagon to the three of them. "Come along now, I don't want you two napping all day. Jane come up here, come see who's walking along with us."

Jane, her face pulled in to its usual downcast scowl, looked out from the canvas cover. "Now come on out here," said her mother, "You could walk along with Maddie for a spell." Jane considered for a moment and then holding the skirt of her dress tightly, slipped over the seat and dropped down next to the wagon.

"Having fun Jane?" I asked, my voice I hoped sounded friendly.

"No," she answered. Jane conserved her words, releasing very few at any one time. We'd been to school together some, and although we were at different levels we couldn't help but see each other in the one-room schoolhouse. She was never much of a scholar, but she did manage to get through school at her own pace.

It was hard to imagine Jane as the Applegate's only daughter. There was none of the good-natured banter about her. She didn't even resemble her parents. They were rose-cheeked and dimpled and rarely lacked a smile. Jane was just plain gray with lips that looked as though they'd been permanently pulled down at the edges and eyebrows that were too heavy. Her eyes looked like they might be gray, not the sparkling kind of gray that twinkled when there was an icy snow in the air, but a gray that you see on a dismal fog-enshrouded day when it looks as though it's never going to clear.

While we were at school, Jane's mother had made all of her dresses from bright gingham, but the colors never seemed to last on Jane, they faded quickly into a nondescript hue until all of her clothing seemed to be of the same drab color. It matched her skin. Mrs. Applegate didn't seem to notice the bland child she had produced. She would babble along merrily and just plain out ignore the long silences of her only daughter.

"Jane, will you write to anyone back home?" I asked. I wasn't real good at making friends but I was determined to have some sort of conversation with the only girl almost my age. It was that or I could go back to listening to Isabelle drone on.

"No," was the only answer forthcoming.

"I haven't anyone to write to except Grams and I'd write to Sadie too, but she can't read."

"Are you going to miss home?" I queried further.

"No," she answered kicking at a stone.

"Oh she does," interjected Mrs. Applegate, sitting high on the wagon. I didn't know she'd been listening.

"She misses her friends and school and the yard where she used to play. Oh my yes, she does miss it some. But she's excited about the move to the West. She's been looking forward to it for some time. She'll meet some nice fella out there and get herself married up. Oh my, yes she will. Git on there Bess," she said snapping the whip on the oxen's rump. "Gotta get us to Oregon, we do."

I looked over at the too thin girl, nearly my age and except for the slouch was just as tall as I was. Hard to see her face with her bonnet pulled so far forward. She had long brownish hair done in tight smooth braids, not at all like mine that were usually sprouting wisps around the edges and always threatening to pop loose of their ties.

We walked along in silence for a while letting the Applegate wagon get ahead of us.

"She doesn't mean to answer for me all the time," said Jane, "It's just her way. She doesn't know what to do with someone like me."

"What do you mean someone like you?" I asked.

"Oh you know, nothing to say and not very interesting."

"But..." I began, not sure what I was going to say.

"Watch it," yelled Jacob from his wagon. I ignored him, he's teasing again - I just knew it. I wasn't even going to turn to let him know I'd heard him.

A warning sound crackled through the air. My hair stood on end. There was an ominous rattle that was too close. We stopped. We froze. I knew that sound, I'd heard it before. A sweat broke out making my armpits damp; I could feel the blood drain from my face. Where was it? I didn't dare look around. It gave its warning rattle again, an agitated, dull and frightening sound. The noise was something like the cicada's chirping to announce the summer heat - only it wasn't a cicada. A gun went off. The rattling stopped almost instantly.

"It's OK," said a voice coming up behind us. Rafferty Jones rode up next to us, his gun still smoking. "You're OK," he said again looking down at me. I'm sure the color was drained from my face.

"I know I am," I said reaching down to pull on my bonnet. I glanced for just a moment to the side of the trail. The nearly six-foot long snake, its body not knowing it was dead, still twirled around itself. For a moment I thought I was going to be sick. The wagon train hadn't even stopped.

"Almost got you he did," said the gravelly voice sounding like pieces of broken shale scrapping against each other. I looked up at the tall man mounted on one of our best horses. "Be mindful of where yer' steppin' girls or you'll be steppin' into trouble."

Rafferty Jones, one of our hired men took a moment to reload. "He's a real big one awright, look at them rattles." We girls shuddered giving the dying snake a wide berth.

Uncle Bert, his horse at a gallop, stopped inches from us. He turned to the slowing wagons, "Go on," he yelled. "It ain't trouble, it's OK." Uncle Bert turned to Rafferty, "So I see you got him with one shot."

"That I did, little early in the year for a rattler that size," he said readjusting his hat lower over his forehead, the one good eye staring out from beneath the brim. I watched a moment longer hard to tell in which direction that one eye was staring.

"Go along girls," said Uncle Bert. "We'll be stopping up by the river; we can all take a break for lunch."

Uncle and I exchanged a quick glance; it had

been a narrow escape. I realized I'd been careless and knew there'd be a lecture coming from Isabelle when she heard of what happened. At least I hadn't been barefoot. I hated wearing shoes, but the ground hadn't warmed up enough yet. So, early this morning I had pulled on my new heavy trail boots.

I was supposed to be grateful for the new boots, but I hated them. They were too big and they were dull coal black with heavy laces going up the front. I wanted brown. And I certainly didn't want boots that went halfway up my leg making it almost impossible to bend.

We continued walking. The idle chatter had stopped as we kept a good eye out. It didn't take much longer to reach the river. We were to stop there for lunch. By the time all the wagons had pulled over, I stopped trembling.

Lunch was quick and easy, just as we'd planned. It was too far to go to take the time for a fire and a hot meal. Instead, there was fresh bread made the day before and what was left of the cold pork from Sadie's mom. She had made more than a two-week supply, if we could just keep it fresh. Bert and David dismounted and joined us for their meal.

"Seems we're off to a good start," said Bert.

"Nice clear trail so far and fair breezes. We'll be up in the Oregon Country before the snows fly for sure."

"It's only April," said Isabelle. "I should certainly hope we arrive long before the snows fly."

"Well now," said Bert, "Can't be too sure of anything what with one thing and 'nother. But we do have a decent trail to follow, that be a blessing. All thanks to the buffalo that used to roam these parts; course that and old Dan'l Boone. We might just have ourselves a real easy trip for a spell. Haven't had to clear away anything yet and haven't seen an Injun."

"Careful Bertram, you're scaring the children," said Isabelle. She only used his Christian name when she wanted his full attention.

"I'm not scared," I said, putting this morning behind me, "What harm could possibly come?"

"Well now girl, there's Injuns, and storms, and rivers to cross, and mountains to climb, and of course snakes," he said winking. There was a silent pact to not mention the morning incident to Isabelle. They'd told the wagons up forward that a gun had discharged accidentally, and so far everyone had been too busy to question it further. I decided to change the subject before Isabelle could question whatever we were talking about.

"When do we get to Independence?" I asked.

"Not for a while yet," Uncle Bert answered with a twinkle in his eye. "It's only been 'bout a couple weeks that we've been on the trail. What's your hurry young Miss?" He and Uncle Dave both looked so much like Father; they could have been triplets instead of brothers. Seeing them both made me miss him all the more.

"No real hurry, just wondering about Father."

"Well now, should be about halfway through June that we'll be in Missouri if I got my figuring right. Only took your Uncle Dave and me about a month traveling on horseback when we came back this way. Now, of course, we've got some baggage."

"You mean us?" asked Jacob.

"That would be the same."

He laughed. "On horseback we had a bedroll, a bit of food and our rifles; it took nothing to cover the miles. Going back now, we've got about eight or ten wagons, a herd of horses, some cows, and God knows how many women and children, and a few men that look as though they've never sat a horse."

Leaning back against the fallen log he inhaled deeply on his pipe, occasionally pointing it, using it for emphasis. "This might be a longer journey then we expected. And I'm thinkin' it's about time to load up. We got us our first river crossing in a few hours."

He stood, knocked the ash from his pipe and yelled first in one direction, then the other: "All up." Tucking his pipe safely in the pocket with the scattered burn holes he mounted the fidgeting gelding.

"Quickly now," said Isabelle as she gathered up the lunch dishes, "We don't want to be the last."

Her scrambling only brought on a fresh bout of coughing, which meant I would have to do the clearing up. Our place was right smack in the middle of the line of wagons. We were the only wagon without a permanent male driver. Jacob was driving the supply wagon. We were going to have to work hard to keep up.

Uncle David would help but chose mostly to ride his saddle horse. That way he was able to go back and forth up and down the line to watch that everything was as it should be. Isabelle tired easily, but we all agreed that I could fill in when needed.

Uncle David tried to help Jacob with the supply wagon too. It wasn't that easy for a fourteen-year-old to control the two oxen, even though he pretended it was nothing. The wagon that we rode in had been kept light so that Isabelle or I could handle it. She also had asked for enough space in the back to sleep.

The other wagon was packed with everything that was left of our life back in Virginia. Everything except my bed and my bureau. It had been decided that there wasn't room for either. We gave them to Sadie. There was room however for Isabelle's blanket chest and for her two trunks.

I knew I was going to have to drive all afternoon; Isabelle just wasn't going to be up to it. I took the reins gingerly. Father and Jacob had hitched up the team back at home to get the oxen accustomed to the yoke and to get the driver accustomed to directing them, but that wasn't any guarantee that things couldn't go wrong. He had taken time to show me how to drive the oxen, but still, I had to work to keep my hands from trembling.

As the afternoon wore on I started to feel more and more comfortable. I'd flick the reins now and again when the oxen seemed to lose attention and would slow down. Odd that Father had taught me how to shoot, but never let me drive the farm wagon or the buckboard. That is until he knew I'd need to know how to drive a covered wagon. Turned out though that the shooting lessons were successful, I was a pretty fine shot, better than Jacob anyway; but then Father had said Jacob's eyes weren't so good.

Isabelle, of course, loathed the idea of a girl with a gun; so we didn't often do it when she was around. Father had said it was necessary that everyone learn 'cause we weren't exactly living in Boston – Isabelle's only home before moving south – the south that she had referred to as the hinterlands. She didn't call our home state the hinterlands when Father was around.

Father liked to point out that what took place in the confines of the fair city of Boston did not include ladies walking on the sidewalks while firing at wild animals. But, I had said to Father that for that exact reason – that this wasn't Boston – I needed to learn. He'd answered with "mind your stepmother." But then while she napped we sometimes would slip off and I would get to fire at the bottles that he set up for me. I learned fairly quickly and was mostly accurate – course Father's hope was that there'd never be a time when I'd need to use it.

THREE

The sun was low in the western sky, as the wagons approached the river crossing. Uncle Bert's horse was pacing nervously through the water, first one-way and then the other. He was choosing his footing carefully as he maneuvered between the rocks. It was the Cumberland River. Uncle Bert and Uncle David had crossed it in the fall. They said it was nothing more than a very wide creek. Course back then they were getting through a long drought. Well, that drought was over. I wouldn't have called it a creek any longer. It was now a rushing torrent of water, icy from the melting snows, cascading down from somewhere up north.

Urging the fidgety horse into the water, they made their way across, as they dodged the branches tumbling end over end. I watched, hardly aware that I was chewing on the end of one of my braids. The water was spilling over the tops of their saddles as the two tried to keep their balance. They were midstream when Uncle Bert nodded to David, a sign to return. The rushing water canceled any hope of discussion.

"Alright then," he said, shaking the water off his jacket. "We'll tackle this in the morning. We'll have time then to stretch a couple of ropes across to get us over." He was deep in thought. "Maybe even go upriver apiece."

It was easy enough to see the concern that was etched around the eyes of the onlookers. "We've done real fine so far, let's not push it." The two brothers pulled on the reins moving away from the gathering.

"I'm ready to go now," Al Roydon said as he dangled the leather straps between his hands. His two sisters-in-law sat ramrod straight by his side, their black skirts spilling over the splintery boards of the wagon seat. We didn't know them real well. They'd been one of the lead wagons for most of the way. He flicked the reins, not waiting for an answer. I watched him raise his whip and bring it down hard across the backs of his oxen. They lurched forward in surprise. Heard tell that was his way, being both impatient and short-tempered.

Uncle Bert turned back to the waiting wagons, "Now wait a minute Al, we're heading into the dark here and we'd be pushing it to get us all across tonight. Seems it'd make more sense to start off early when the animals are fresh."

"I'm goin' now," he said. "Get out of my way."

Uncle Bert scratched at his beard, "Suit yer'self," he said, "but it's likely you'll be goin' alone."

Al cracked his whip again on the backs of his four oxen. The snap was so loud the two spinsters sitting beside him winced, their skirts rustling.

"Al," began his wife, peeking out from between the folds of canvas, "Is this wise?"

"Leave me be woman," he answered, none too friendly, "You can come or stay, suit yer self."

She disappeared back into the wagon. "You two wanna come?" he asked his wife's two older sisters. They sat squeezed together, their skirts blending into a cascade of black.

I watched. I knew little of the sisters, only that Anne, much younger than the two older maiden ladies, had married Al Roydon rather suddenly before they'd left. And that Anne had begged her two sisters, Victoria and Elizabeth, to come with her. There was a stony silence that surrounded their wagon except when Al Roydon had something to say. Then it was usually an order barked at someone.

"Well," he said, "You comin'?" The sisters nodded, their hands folded tightly in their laps, their backs tense, mouths in a grim line. "Then we're off. See you on the other side," he said to Bert.

"Right," said Bert, "Ladies," he said touching the brim of his hat.

From the moment the wagon rolled into the water, it was wrong. Al started from a place further downstream from where the Uncles had tried to cross. The water was lapping at the bottom of the wagon after only a few feet. We watched from shore in horror as the oxen struggled to keep their heads above the rushing water. They bellowed a frantic cry, the muscles on their shoulders tensing, as their legs frantically reached out for solid ground. Al struck the animals again and again with his whip.

"Get on now," he yelled over and over. I never did see the necessity of hitting an animal. I winced every time I heard the crack of his whip.

I could see Anne peering out of the back of the wagon her hands gripping the splintery boards, it looked like there were tears sliding down her cheeks.

The two uncles, both mounted, saw what was about to happen as the wagon swayed and began to be pushed down the river. The twins looked at each other and together galloped into the water, their mounts shivered as the iciness engulfed them.

No words were needed as each man guided his horse to a side of the oxen. The brothers spoke encouraging words to their mounts – experienced or not, the whites of the eyes of those two horses bulged with an unspeakable terror. They swam when their hooves no longer touched bottom. David came around the back going to the far side. Bert urged his horse to the side up river. Together they grabbed the oxen's tether and pulled and guided them until they once again gained their footing.

The wagon swayed again as a branch slammed against it. Al Royden slashed again and again with his whip, the oxen bawled, but the branch had lodged in the spokes of one of the wheels, locking it in place. The wagon began to tip as we watched in horror. One of the sister's slid off the seat. It happened so fast. She was over the side into the icy water. The other sister screamed in terror. There was no way to stop it; she was being swept down the river. Four of the men mounted on shore galloped into the water.

Bert grabbed at the branch trying to pull it

from where it was locked in the wagon wheel. David held tight to the oxen. Bert couldn't get a good grip on the branch. His foot came out of the stirrup and with one last effort he kicked out with a tremendous force. There was a loud crack. The branch was broken. It released the wheel.

The four riders were traveling downstream trying to catch up with the black bombazine skirt that bobbed up and down through the rapids. An arm reached up out of the depths, the hand clawlike. The rushing of the water drowned out the screams and cries of the women watching from the shore.

Anne looked as though she was going to jump out of the back of the wagon. But instead had her hand covering her mouth in disbelief. Her other hand trying to hold her steady gripped the wagon to keep from being tossed out too. The river traveled out of sight between the trees. The light was fading. The patch of black disappeared in the rushing water.

Angry words came from the other side of the river. Al's voice rose in agitation. Uncle Bert rarely raised his voice, but now spared nothing in his tongue lashing of Al Royden. Although the words couldn't be distinguished over the noise of the river, we knew he was about as riled as he'd ever been.

The wagons circled. We were unusually quiet. Dinner fires were started; it seemed that even the young ones made little noise. As we washed up the last of the supper dishes, the four riders came back into camp. They just shook their heads. They dismounted and said nothing. Guess one of the sisters is lost forever may God rest her soul.

The fires died down, the horses were tethered. It was the first casualty on the trail. I'd heard not everyone made it all the way through to the west. But I didn't want to think about it.

Uncle Bert came by to say good night. "Head further upstream in the morning," he said. "Water's more shallow. Not so treacherous." He shook his head and walked off.

A hush fell over the camp with only an occasional hoot from an owl. His lonely cry echoed through the darkness.

FOUR

Odd how quickly we'd settled into a routine. It was already June. The days were longer and so warm that we walked without shawls. The trail continued to be passable. There were still forests and huge rocks to get around, but we were managing. Uncle Bert said it had once been a buffalo trail and the Indians had used it too, probably not so long ago. I had become accustomed to walking beside the wagons and rarely tired. Most often I would stay by one of the others so's I wouldn't have to be under Isabelle's watchful eye.

She seemed to be getting better, although she was still thin as a fence post. Her coughing fits were further apart so I only had to drive the wagon occasionally. She liked being up there on that high seat, being in control of two lumbering beasts. 'Course she didn't like what it was doing to her once soft white hands. But in truth, I think she preferred to be up on the seat alone or with just Hannah. I'm thinking I may be too much of a trial to her and she'd prefer not to have me around all the livelong day vexing her with all my bad habits.

Father had said Isabelle loves you all and just wants to help and to teach you three children proper manners. Before he left, he said he trusted us to behave properly and not make him ashamed. I sure wish he were with us now. Things always seemed right when he was nearby. Isabelle didn't go correcting me all the livelong day when he was there; she pretty much would let me be. Now without him here, I'm almost like her pet project – needing constant correction and to be endlessly bossed around.

What seemed to work best was my walking next to the Applegate wagon or even up by the Cantrell's. Abigail Cantrell is just 17 years old and she's stuck up and likes to lord it over me that she's older, but sometimes it's either talk to her or talk to myself. I've about given up on Jane Applegate. We walk together sometimes, but I always babble like a fool when I'm with her. The silences are sometimes so long, so I just talk away. Once in awhile she nods or looks at me out from under her bonnet, sometimes in disbelief at some of the things I say. Like the time I said I wonder how many of us will make it through.

This wasn't a journey for ladies who wore lace gloves and played the pianoforte. I knew that much. At the meetings they had before we left, they were very clear that this wasn't for the weak. There were all sorts of hazards. Some people turned back and others didn't make it through. 'Course they didn't talk about why they didn't make it through – but I knew.

I sure wish Sadie was with me, she'd been my only friend at home. Isabelle couldn't wait to get us apart. Being from Boston, Isabelle likes to pretend that slavery doesn't exist. She calls it an abomination and the scourge of mankind. If she was so opposed to the difference, why'd she use Sadie's mom so often to come and clean the house and do the gardening? And why'd she turn up her nose whenever Sadie and I would go off to play together? 'Course that didn't happen too often what with all the chores we had to do.

Father had freed Sadie's whole family before he set off for the West. It was best he said. We couldn't afford to take them with us and he'd been intending to free them for a while. It just all fell into place.

"Put your bonnet on young lady or you're going to get so brown you'll look like a wild Indian," Isabelle called down. She sometimes had eyes in the back of her head, which was a real annoyance. And then sometimes it was just easier to do what she said rather than argue with her. I wanted to ask her how many blonde and blue-eyed Indians she'd ever seen. But Father had said don't rile her; we were lucky he said to have her for our new mother.

Wish he'd asked me about that before he'd chosen her. I wondered sometimes if it would ever settle right with me. Mother died just five years ago, I'd been about ten at the time and never felt like I'd really known her, she'd been sick so often. And here was Isabelle to take her place.

"Wait up." It was Brian McElhinney. He slid off his horse and looked like he wanted to walk for a while. He'd done it before; I think he was sweet on stuck-up Abigail Cantrell.

"Hi," I said, pretending enthusiasm. We still had hours ahead of us 'til camp and it would be more interesting to talk with him than to babble away at Jane Applegate.

"What's up?" he asked.

"Well tonight I'll be going to a dance, and to-morrow I'll be having a fitting for my new riding outfit and then…"

"Hold on now, what's the problem?"

"Nothing," I answered, "Just plain out bored I

guess."

"Hey, you're doing fine," he said. "It's going to be a long trip, may as well try to enjoy some of it."

"Yeah, like what?"

"Hey," he said, "You didn't used to be like this. What's going on?"

"Whatdaya mean I didn't used to be like this?"

"Well now, when Randy was alive didn't we used to have some fun? Like, remember sneaking away and swimming in the creek when we were supposed to be doing chores? And remember when your father would try to teach us all how to shoot?"

"Yeah, I remember." I kicked at a stone, then wished I hadn't. I was barefoot and had been feeling such freedom. Now my toe was throbbing and I wished I'd put on my boots.

"You miss him don't you?" he asked.

I knew who he was talking about. Brian and I had one thing in common; we missed Randy so much it was as if we could see the hole in each other's hearts. No one else ever talked about him. It was as if Brian and I were the only two on the face of the whole earth who had even known him. He was everything I wasn't – he laughed, he was always happy, I'm sure he was Father's favorite and he was almost always poking fun at something. He wasn't at all like Jacob, the serious and always doing-the-right-thing younger brother.

His real name was Randall but anyone who knew him called him Randy. He'd been Brian's best friend and my older brother. He somehow took mother's place when she died. He watched out for me, we were best friends. Now, no one else ever even talked about him.

It was as if he'd never been. As if there was this mysterious blank place in my heart that had no business being there 'cause the person who'd put it there had never existed. The few times that I met up with Brian he would always turn the conversation to Randy. Wasn't sure if I liked that or not. Sometimes I just thought let sleeping dogs lie as Father said so many times. But this sleeping dog wasn't happy lying still and every now and again would get up to nip at me and remind me that he had been part of my life. He'd died too young and too soon. And there was still a mystery surrounding it. He'd been shot. I didn't like to think about it 'cause they never found out how it happened or why.

"So Brian," I said, trying to focus on something else, "Heard that Abigail Cantrell was planning on settling up by your family in Oregon."

"Might be true," he answered. "Didn't know they had made up their minds yet."

"Maw wants you," yelled a young boy who was running towards Brian. The similarity of the two was striking; I thought that little one looks just like a copy of Brian, just shorter. But then, the entire family looked like that, like they were quintuplets only different sizes. They had dark blue eyes and sandy, perfectly straight hair. They each had a case of freckles that they seemed to grow out of at some particular age and they all had a small gap between their front teeth. You could pick those five brothers out of a crowd.

Father had said once that they had two girls after Brian but they'd both died from scarlet fever when they were very young and ever since then the McElhinneys could only produce boys. Now there were five of them in the family.

"What's she want Sean Patrick," he asked as he swung himself back up into the saddle.

"Didn't say, 'cept you better come quick." Sean Patrick didn't seem to be able to say anything unless he yelled, which he was doing now. Isabelle said he was probably hard of hearing and didn't even know he was yelling. Isabelle said it happened sometimes when people had gotten the measles.

"I'm comin," he said. He tipped his hat to me; that made me feel funny, old maybe. I'm not sure. Only men my father's age had ever tipped their hats to me and that was mostly when I was with Father.

I continued on trying to decide whether or not to climb up in the wagon and pull my boots on before Isabelle noticed. I decided against it. Wish I could've ridden a horse like the wranglers did or Jacob and the other boys, but as with most things Isabelle said it would be unseemly. We didn't have a sidesaddle with us and I didn't want to explain to her that I'd been riding astride horses since I had learned how to walk. After all, we were raising horses at our farm and it would be highly unlikely that one of us couldn't ride.

I'd get back to it as soon as we settled in Oregon. I had ridden most of the dozen horses that we were bringing with us, some of them bareback, which even Father disapproved of. I missed riding, a lot, and wasn't even allowed to help the wranglers drive them along. Somehow it couldn't come soon enough, our getting to the Oregon Country.

The wagon train was slowing and then came to a stop. Isabelle must have been dozing 'cause she very nearly ran our wagon into the backend of the Barnes's wagon.

"Hold up." It was Uncle Bert. It was too early to be stopping. The sun had a ways to go before the darkness canceled our day.

"What's up?" I asked Uncle David as he rode past.

"Lost a boy," he answered. "Need some help here," he yelled. "Boy's lost."

It took minutes only to get together six mounted men to go back along the trail. Didn't take long to figure out who it was. Mrs. McElhinney could be heard for the entire length of the train. She was bawling and carrying on something terrible. It was her Ryan, Brian's five-year-old brother. No one seemed to know where he'd gotten off to or how long he'd been gone. He'd been seen at breakfast but we hadn't stopped at lunch 'cause there were rain clouds gathering and we'd wanted to cover some territory before it commenced.

The children would often walk or ride with different wagons. They all seemed to turn up and appear at the right campfires at suppertime so there didn't seem to be much call to worry during the day. We all kept a good eye out for each other. We saw Indians occasionally, off in the distance, but Uncle David said there more'n likely wouldn't be a problem in this area. I think he didn't want to scare us 'cause that's not what I heard.

Some remnants of what was left of the tribes of the Osage were still around and it was said they weren't any too friendly. There weren't all that many left after the government took their land when they tried to relocate them to somewhere where they'd never been - and didn't want to be. Heard they still weren't happy and the few who were left weren't real pleased with the wagon trains that kept coming. I did notice that there was now a watch posted each night.

"Have you seen him?" asked Brian. I shook my head no, but kept searching the horizon. Ryan usually walked along the side of the wagons. Seemed that when he got tired one or the other of the wranglers or his older brothers would take him up on their horse. Now it seemed that no one could account for him since early this morning. Uncle Bert stayed back and said we may as well circle up for the night, we probably wouldn't be going anywhere for awhile.

I felt a chill crawl up my back. It wasn't a nice feeling. Since losing one of the sisters to the river, we'd had no bad luck at all 'cept of course for the Barnes ox that broke his leg. Broke it so bad they had to shoot it. They took one of the three that were left and took him off the yoke and were now operating with just a pair.

Course that meant they had to lighten their load some and it was a sorry day for Miz Barnes when she watched them unload her bedstead and bureau and what looked like a real heavy dry sink. They left it all at the side of the trail. There were other pieces of furniture and trunks too that had been abandoned. Guess maybe others realized they were never going to make it with the loads they wanted their team of oxen or mules to haul.

Miz Barnes added her things to the scattered pieces already there, which included a table with a broken leg and two chairs with badly peeling red paint. There was a mirror there too, which I would have liked to have, but a crack went from one corner to the other. Nevertheless, it'd been awhile since I'd seen any likeness of myself. I stood for a moment peering into the glass. The reflected image was wavy and it was hard to tell, but it looked like I was taller than I remembered. Maybe even more filled out, but it may have just been the ill-fitting dress I was wearing. Not sure if I liked what I saw. The face seemed sad even though it was hard to tell who was looking back at me. I saw as much as I wanted and turned back to see Miz Barnes who was using her apron to wipe at the tears dripping off her chin.

They said her furniture had come all the way from Connecticut. Mr. Barnes' parents had brought it down with them when they moved to Virginia. Mr. Barnes told his wife he'd try to come back and get it. Somehow we all knew that wasn't going to happen.

Well sometimes there's an upside to things 'cause after they shot that ox with the broken leg, we all had stewed or roasted ox for a week. Meant that the men didn't have to take so much time hunting every other day.

Most nights we all gathered at our own fires and had quiet dinners. Often there was bantering back and forth and the little ones would scurry between the wagons playing tag or hide and seek while we made dinner. But tonight there was quiet. By the time our meals had been gotten together, the rain had started. We had to eat inside our wagons sitting on our blankets. It was a whole lot easier than stringing up a piece of canvas so's we could stay dry.

It was never fun trying to clean up, but in the rain, it was worse. And, of course, Isabelle had one of her coughing fits again, so I had to do it all. I could have erected a tarp or something, but somehow it just seemed easier to just get drenched while I cleaned up the dishes.

By the time I was done the rain was coming down so hard, it had doused the fire. I was soaked through. There was nothing to do but get back into the wagon and change into a dry shift. I wouldn't be sleeping in my usual place tonight. Most nights I liked to sleep outside, but when it got this wet it was near impossible. I'd already been woken up a couple of nights when I had to scramble up into the wagon to get out of the puddles.

At breakfast, the men hadn't come back. It was still drizzly and gray so no one objected when we served cold beans and cold cornbread. We parceled it out in the wagon so's we wouldn't have to go out and get sloshing wet again. The Uncles seemed to miss their coffee most. Isabelle certainly was not known for her coffee making skills. She drank tea, and only tea, and couldn't be bothered trying to understand how one can brew up a proper kettle of coffee. She said coffee was the drink of barbarians. That was when I decided I'd start drinking coffee. Mine still wasn't quite as flavorful as what Sadie's mom used to make back at home, but it was passable.

Whenever possible the Uncles would stop by

another campfire when they smelled a fresh pot brewing. Abigail Cantrell took great pride in her cooking and knew that the smell of her fresh brewed coffee attracted the men - like bees to honey. It was almost funny watching them make fools of themselves over her special brew, tipping their hats, and saying "Good Evening Miz Cantrell." And then her reply, so sticky sweet with her big cow eyes "Oh Sir, would you care to sit and enjoy a fresh cup of coffee?" She had Brian hooked all right. Whenever his parents didn't need him, that's where he could be found! Can't really blame him actually with four younger brothers always hanging around him and Brian being the oldest.

"Uncle Bert will they be back soon?" I was tired of the rain and I was tired of waiting for the men to return from their hunt for Brian's little brother. Where could he have gotten off to? I keep expecting him to pop up in someone's wagon from where he'd been hiding.

"Maddie, we've got to be patient just a while longer. We'll break camp soon as they're back. 'Spect it won't be too long." But it was. It was nearly sundown, had there been a sun. It was still raining so hard it was difficult to tell what time of day it was. But I was hungry so suspected it must be getting close to dinner.

I was returning from the stream with a bucket of water as the six horsemen trotted back into camp. Their hats were pulled low, their collars pulled up to their cheekbones. All that could be seen on each was a pair of eyes staring out. Uncle David's eyes didn't have the usual crinkles in the corners.

He dismounted and walked over to Brian. They spoke in low voices as I strained to hear what they were saying. A few words drifted over to our wagon like Injuns, lost, bears and wolves. I knew it wasn't good. Isabelle pulled me back into the wagon.

"You're going to catch your death hanging out in the rain like that." She said it between fits of coughing.

Supper was again a ragtag affair. More cold beans and we still had some ox left, cooked from a few nights ago. It wasn't really looking very appealing. We each got to chew on some dried apple. There weren't many slices left and we were still a ways from St. Louis where we'd be able to set in some supplies.

Mrs. McElhinney screamed and carried on for most of the night. My only thought was that if Ryan had been within five miles he would've heard and come running home. He was only five years old was all I could think. No one seemed to want to talk about it. We left at sunup; Brian held back, he said he would catch up.

FIVE

We crossed the Mississippi today. Almost couldn't see the other side. Never saw a river like that back in Virginia. They say it might be the biggest river we're ever going to see.

We had to cross by ferry and it took most of the day: first the wagons, then the horses and then the cattle. The ferryman said we were lucky 'cause the rains hadn't been too heavy up this way and the river was calm. Uncle David said he was robbing us by charging us two bits for each boatload. The ferryman seemed just ripe for an argument when he answered Uncle David: "It be one bit over and one bit back."

Jacob who couldn't keep still said, "Yeah, but we're not coming back."

"Well I am," he answered and spit a half wad of chewed up tobacco real close to Jacob's boot. "And it's gonna cost you one bit to get me back."

Jacob came to the wagon to dig out the money box and took out enough to get us across. "Got no choice," he said. "There's no other way to get to the other side."

Uncle Bert had said that the Mississippi was gonna' be some river. Well, I'll tell you, it made the Ohio look like a backwater creek.

Hannah was on my lap for one of our conversations where I did all the talking. "Look Hannah, look at the boats, there must be hundreds." I was exaggerating of course but I wanted her to pull her eyes out from under my apron. It worked.

"Now just lookit there. Trappers." There were three canoes coming so close to us we could see everything they'd packed into them. It was mostly blankets and furs and a metal pot or two. The trappers had heavy black beards and as warm as it was they were wearing coonskin hats. They were dark skinned and a bit frightening. A couple of them waved to us and called out words, which I'm quite sure were French. We smiled and waved back. There were Indians too, paddling by. One small canoe passed close in front of us. "Hannah, look. See the papoose? And look how they strapped that baby in, bet you wouldn't put up with that." She hid her head again. "They're not scary; we've seen lots of them. Uncle Bert says just leave them be and they mind their own business."

He also said that every now and again they'd find a horse or cow missing, but in this part of the country, the Indians weren't much of a problem. We'd have to mind our P's and Q's though after we pulled away from Independence. That was where we'd have our next big river crossing.

We had such a nice view of the water sitting up on the wagon seat. Isabelle was in the back and looked as though she was going to puke.

"Look Hannah, your Momma isn't too happy." She perked up at this and looked back in the wagon to see her stepmother, sitting on the mattress, her arms locked around her knees drawn up close to her chest. "She won't sit with us," I said fearing I was going to get the giggles. She looked so funny with her eyes squeezed tight.

"It's OK Hannah, she just doesn't like the water. Now look over there, it's another ferry and it's bigger than this one, he has two wagons on it, but we're faster. See Jacob over there. He's waiting for us. He already has the supply wagon across."

The ferry moved up and down with the gentle motion of the water. An occasional wave broke over the splintery wood. The wagon swayed. With the creak of the wheels and the unsteady bobbing, I wondered if the ropes were strong enough to hold us on the few pieces of rough-hewn lumber.

It didn't look any too sturdy.

"We're almost there." By the time we reached shore, Hannah was looking all around, about as curious as any five-year-old could be. We landed with a thump. I breathed a sigh of relief as Jacob hitched up the oxen. Isabelle was still huddled in the back as I drove the wagon off. She was real glad to slide back up on the seat once we made it to dry land.

Crossing the Mississippi meant we're done with all the hills and valleys of Kentucky and we'd made it to Missouri. Uncle David said if the weather holds we'll be in Independence by the end of June. It's not halfway yet, but it's where many of the wagons connect with others to travel in a caravan. It's said it's safer that way as there's so much unknown ahead. It would be a treat to have some others with us. Maybe some other girls to talk to or walk with would be nice. The endless day after day walking does get boring.

It seems it's been so long since we departed. I wonder if life will ever settle down. Will we ever live in a house again or is this my life: beans and cornbread and greasy bacon with choking dust and endless trails and wagons that break down too often? We have another few days 'til we get up to Independence. Maybe we'll be able to spend some time there while we provision.

The weather changed from damp to a drenching summer heat. We'd left the coolness of Kentucky behind and now it was so hot, Uncle Bert pulled us over early and had us circle up. We had a dinner of bacon and cold cornbread with what little butter we had, and munched on the last of the apple slices. My favorite, but very few left. Isabelle and Sadie's mom had dried a huge amount last fall from the apples we collected. Guess we'd been eating too many 'cause now they were just about gone.

The butter churn has given us lots of butter after the rough ride in the wagon. Well, most times. Today's ride had been tame and the churn gave us little. Now I could either spend my night plunging the dasher up and down to make more butter come or I could skim off what we had and drink the milk that hadn't turned. I chose to let us all have as much as we wanted of the warmish milk. The few cows that we were driving would yield more later.

It was so hot that we all retired to stretch out on our quilts as the sun went down. I listened as Isabelle tossed and turned and couldn't seem to get comfortable. It must have been a lot hotter up in the wagon than it was sleeping on the ground.

"Maddie, where are you?" For a moment I thought about changing my name. Maybe just for the rest of this trip, so I didn't have to hear it so often - especially when it was followed by an order.

"I'm here." Crawling out of my jumbled nest of quilts from under the wagon, I made my way towards the sound of the coughing. The night had been so hot and I couldn't get comfortable either so was almost glad to leave my hideout.

"Could you please fetch me a drink of water?" Her coughing hadn't really gotten much worse it was just louder.

Most nights she had a pail of water in the wagon for herself and Hannah, but there must not have been any left. There was no breeze and not a puff of fresh air and my shift felt scratchy and too long.

"I'll get it," I answered. We weren't that far from the Mississippi and there were lots of little creeks around. It wouldn't be far to get a bucket of water. Usually, we watched for each other whenever we left the circle of wagons, but it was late and by the sounds of the snoring, everyone was too far into sleep to pay me any mind. Most often there was a guard posted, but who knew where he was.

The moon threw just enough light to find my way down to the creek, that and the sound of the burbling of the water. It felt so peaceful to be down there, it was quiet and a little cooler and I couldn't resist putting my feet in. An owl hooted from high in a tree. I sat on a flat stone and splashed, it felt so good. The pebbles on the bottom were smooth and cool and were soothing on feet that had walked too many miles. The cool wet felt wonderful.

No one was around, the moon was sparkling off the ripples and I couldn't hold back. I hadn't been swimming since last year – wasn't proper said Isabelle. We ladies could all bathe together on the trail when there was a fresh source of water, but there would be no swimming, that was for boys.

I made my way out to the middle where it wasn't even over my head. I floated for a while and then did a few quiet strokes up the creek and then back down. A bunch of ducks broke the silence with their quaking. It gave me a start. I hadn't meant to disturb them.

I realized the moon's light wasn't quite enough to show me where I'd come out of the trees. I squinted into the dark, searching the shoreline and just when I thought I was going to have to yell for help, I saw a bit of light from the moon reflecting off my bucket. I realized I'd been gone far too long.

The water had felt so good, I hadn't bathed in so long but I had to get back. My shift clung to me as I walked back out of the water. I filled the bucket and reached down to wring out the hem of my shift. From out of nowhere, a hand was slapped over my mouth, an arm that felt like a hot piece of thick iron squeezed around my waist.

My mind couldn't understand what was happening. I thought I would pass out from fright. There was no opportunity to scream or kick. Whoever it was, he was a monster. His breath came in hot gasps on my neck. It smelled like old stale whiskey. His arm was crushing me around my middle and it felt like my teeth were going to come loose from the huge hairy hand that was squeezing my mouth shut. He was holding me so tight I couldn't breathe. I was going to suffocate and die I just knew it. He was carrying me into the woods. Wait I wanted to scream. I need to get the bucket. Who knows where that thought came from?

I tried to kick out but my feet felt like they were hitting iron. We had almost reached the woods, when I heard an awful thud like a watermelon being smashed by a board, and then almost in slow motion, like he had to think about it, he released his hold on me and I dropped to the ground. I looked up at the biggest man I'd ever seen.

"Mon Dieu," he said over and over, each time getting fainter. He was French. Maybe one of the trappers but I didn't want to stay to find out.

He staggered and put a large very hairy hand on the back of his head. The red flannel shirt couldn't hide the dripping blood. His coonskin hat had dropped to the ground. A bowie knife on his belt glistened in the moonlight.

"Quick Madison, run." Well, I didn't have to be told twice. I ran and I knew who was behind me. I'd recognize that cough anywhere and it was keeping up with me. We yelled like a passel of wild Indians and in no time at all, we were circled by most of those formerly sleeping residents of all those wagons.

Isabelle bent over as she tried to stop coughing so hard. She dropped the log she'd used on that trapper's head. How had she picked up something that big and then hit that giant with it? I was impressed. It took a few minutes to catch my breath to try to tell the story.

Everyone crowded around, their eyes wide when I realized I was standing there in my soaking wet shift practically naked. I guess I realized it when I saw Rafferty Jones's one eye staring at me. The light from the dying fire reflected off that one eye and it looked like sparks were leaping off it.

Someone brought a quilt and threw it over me; I think it was Brian. Uncle David and Uncle Bert, in one leap, had mounted their horses and headed down to the stream. Wasn't much they could do though in the dark. Jacob came up and said, "come sleep in my wagon, don't want to frighten Hannah and by the looks of you, you'd frighten a ghost."

"I'm alright," I said but I was already starting to shake and feel some twinges from where he'd squeezed me so tight. During the night I stuck my toe out a couple of times to touch Jacob just to make sure he was there. Sometimes he wasn't too bad for a younger brother.

The morning came much too soon.

SIX

It was the fifteenth of July when we arrived in Independence, Missouri. Uncle Bert called a halt to our parade of wagons and said we could stay four days for repairs and provisioning. It seemed a bit calmer than St. Louis. Someone had said St. Louis was having growing pains with all the Irish and German immigrants. Seems they had a famine in Ireland and many were starving because of a potato disease and thousands were coming to America to survive. We hadn't stayed there long enough to get an understanding of who was there. The Uncles said get to Independence then we could take a few days to rest. They thought provisioning might be better there as it was like a meet up place for all the travelers who would be heading to different destinations like Santa Fe or Texas or Oregon Country.

Many of our wagons could use some attention with spokes and axles and wheels that needed re-pairing. Our animals too could use a few days off to heal their sores. The yokes had done their damage, rubbing and chaffing their shoulders practically down to the bone. As often as we put bacon grease and herbs on their necks and shoulders they were hard to keep clean. The flies would actually lay their eggs in the open wounds. They'd hatch into maggots. Uncle David said leave it, the maggots were the best cleaning tool known. "Injuns do it all the time, works like magic." I didn't want to be the one to argue, so let it be.

We'd been on the trail nearly three months and had made better time than Uncle Bert had imagined. Maybe we were all better pioneers than he knew and here we were in an actual town for a few days. Well, not really a town. It was more like a bunch of buildings thrown together, with lots still being built. But there was a wide dirt road going down the middle with all kinds of stores. It was the best we'd seen so far.

There was such an odd assortment of people too; I suppose that was why the Uncles had us camp outside of town. It looked like a riotous place, lots bigger than where we were coming from in Virginia, but not quite as civilized.

"Madison," called Isabelle, her coughing shook the wagon.

"I'm here."

"You're going to have to go to the Post Office to see if there's any word from your father. I believe I'll stay put for the day."

"But he's not expecting us for another month at least."

"Nevertheless, we need to see if he's written with any instructions."

I wasn't going to argue. This was my chance to get away from the wagons to be by myself for awhile.

"Take a few pennies from the box. You may need them." I lifted the top off the barrel of cornmeal and ran my fingers through the yellow meal 'til I located the wooden box. It had my mother and father's initials on it with the date they were married. I had seen Isabelle run her fingers over the carved out engraving and wondered again why she seemed to not mind that there had been someone else in father's life before her. She seemed to know an awful lot about my real mother but only rarely spoke of her. Now and again she'd say something that even my father didn't seem to know about. Like a certain dress she wore when she was young or that her favorite food was gingerbread. Maybe because they were both from Boston, I wasn't sure.

"You'll need to take Jacob," she said, her voice

going down to a whisper. She slumped back on the pillows. I could act like I hadn't heard that last part. She coughed hard into her handkerchief. There were flecks of blood on the snow-white linen. I turned away, pretending I hadn't seen it.

Don't know how she'd gotten this bad. Seemed like it had been a lot worse though since that time when she came out in the middle of the night to save me. The sound of that log when she hit the trapper on the head would always be with me. She'd hit that trapper for all she was worth, and then together we ran like the wind to get as far away from him as possible. It took its toll, she'd been mostly riding in the back of wagon ever since.

I didn't want to disobey, but I set off for town. I could find the Post Office on my own and I was sure I could make it back before she even noticed. I did look around for Jacob, but he wasn't nearby, so left without him. It wasn't much of a walk to town so I knew it'd be all right.

The town was crowded. There were people everywhere. I stopped two ladies with parasols who were holding their skirts high acting as though a brush against anything or anyone would spell certain death. They looked at me as though I were some sort of annoyance or some sort of vermin that the cat had dragged in the back door. So I repeated my question: "Excuse me please, could you tell me where the Post Office is located?"

"Well right there in front of you." They both sniffed, their noses held high. They flounced off. How rude I thought and then looked down at my dress. I realized I must be a sight, faded dress, nearly outgrown; I was bursting out of the top and it had gotten far too short. The black leather boots were scuffed and it was hard to imagine that they'd ever been new. My bonnet was back in the wagon and I was sure my hair must have been sprouting out in every direction. No time to worry about that. The Post Office was just across the road.

Getting there was going to be another thing. I stepped off the wood sidewalk and was nearly knocked over by a wagon. It was filled to the brim with beaver pelts. The driver never even saw me. Trying to avoid the biggest puddles, I had to dodge a few horsemen and then steer around two Indians standing like statues wrapped in ragged blankets. Their eyes took in everything.

So much dust, noise, and confusion. I'd never seen the like. It was a relief to get inside the cool interior of the Post Office. Sure enough, there was a letter waiting. I held it close and tried to imagine my father as he sat down to write to us. I wanted to hurry to get back to the wagon train to read it. The day was already cooling with the sun sinking in the west.

But, I decided, the letter could wait. The freedom of being away from everyone was more than I could believe. If I could browse through one of the shops and maybe be able to tell Isabelle what was there for purchase, I'm sure she'd approve.

Where to go first? There was a general store, a feed store, a trading post - maybe for furs and pelts? And then a stable where it looked like the road ended. There was a haberdasher and a dress shop with three gaily printed dresses hanging in the windows. A building that looked like it had recently been constructed sat in the center of the town. COURTHOUSE was emblazoned over the front entrance. And then a sprawling hotel near the blacksmith shop had a sign in a window that said "Tea." Wouldn't that be a nice treat?

I would have been happy to spend the whole day here. If I moved quickly, maybe I could get to each of the shops. It took no time to wind my way back across the road to begin my exploration. The goods that they had were wonderful. I'd never seen so many interesting things to buy. The general store had hard candy and maple syrup and bolts of gingham and buttons and cheeses and chocolate. I had to touch almost everything. There was a Godey's Lady's Book in the corner that I looked through. It was hard not to covet a pair of the fine boots that had the decorative laces up the front.

"Anything I can help you with young miss?" asked the shopkeeper. I told him no, not yet, just wanted to see what all he had. When I was going round the shop for the fourth or fifth time, the shopkeeper announced to all who were there, "We'll be closing soon, so pick out what you need to buy."

I looked out the window and realized it was almost dark and it had started to rain. Racing out the door, I let it slam behind me. I stopped a minute to get my bearings and turned to head south down the sidewalk. As I stepped off the end, I realized I'd gone the wrong way.

"Drat." I crossed the road – now not so busy, but there were puddles to dodge and ruts not to stumble in. Stepping up onto the sidewalk, I stood in the front of the busiest place in town. A huge sign hung over the door with one word - Saloon. The door was open just a crack. There was lots of noise and laughter spilling out to the sidewalk. It was hard not to look as the swinging doors were pushed open. That was where all the fun was.

"Well look who we have here. Hello young Miss, would ya' be interested in a drink maybe? I could fix ya' up right nice." I turned quickly and moved away keeping my head down. I pretended not to hear him. The boots were thumping behind me, one step to my two.

"Young miss, I just wanted to make yer acquaintance," said the voice behind me. A grimy hand grabbed my arm and whirled me around. "I saw you peeking in, thought mayhap you wanted to stop in for a drink."

"Unhand me Sir," I said using my strongest voice.

A sneer snuck up on one side of his unshaven face, his breath reeked of drink. His eyes seemed to take in all of me. He leaned his head down bringing his face much too close.

"You heard her. Unhand her now."

The glassy eyes turned to see who was doing the speaking and looked into the hard ice blue eyes of Brian. "Remove your hand from the lady. Now."

The fingers, one by one pulled away from my arm. "Just trying to make her acquaintance," he said. "No harm intended."

"Well be on your way then." He said, his eyes flashed a menacing look.

The man tipped his hat, "Good evening to ya' then," he said and staggered off.

Brian took my elbow, "You've got to watch yourself Maddie," he said. I tried to keep my arm from shaking but it wouldn't stop. He drew me closer so that I leaned into him as we made our way down the sidewalk. "What are you doing in town alone?" he asked. "You shouldn't be here without your brother."

"I couldn't find him," I said. That was a half-truth; I hadn't actually looked for him. "I had to go to the Post Office. Oh my gosh, the letter."

"What letter?"

"I had a letter from Father. Where is it? Oh my gosh what'd I do with it."

We looked. We looked until it was so dark we couldn't see a thing and the drizzle had soaked us both. I had to get back to the wagon.

Isabelle was sleeping on our return. We told no one. But the next day very early I went back with Jacob. We stopped at the dry goods store, but they hadn't seen it. Then we thought we found it next to the wood planked sidewalk but weren't real sure. There was a square envelope in a puddle that had soaked all night and then trod upon and what little was left was - all the ink had run off. There was nothing left to read. There would be no letter from Father. I had to tell Isabelle. Not sure why, but for whatever reason, she chose to ignore the loss and not get after me too badly. But you could see it in her eyes.

That night I curled up on my blanket thinking of home and how I missed it. I remembered the hot summer nights when we would sit on the porch and drink lemonade after a long day with the horses. I could almost hear the crunching sound that the rocking chairs made when they rocked back and forth over the peeling paint. Not for the first time, I thought, maybe this isn't for me. Maybe I should turn around and go back.

Tears welled up. I tried to picture my real mother, but her image had faded so long ago, I couldn't bring her up to my mind's eye anymore. I could recall the lingering scent of soap, which seemed to cling to her hands and a bit of her soft singing voice but that was all.

If only Father hadn't had to do this. If only he hadn't gotten it into his head that he needed to be part of the great rush westward. More land he said. Virginia was getting some crowded. We need to break free and move on. It was becoming stifling where we lived with all those newcomers.

His dream had been to raise horses but he'd never been able to keep more than fifteen or so at any one time. He wanted to spread out. Oregon Country he said. But that wasn't even part of the United States. It was under British rule. I'd learned that at school. So exactly how would we do this and would we come under British rule? And hadn't we broken away from that not so long ago? But I'd gotten into trouble more than once with my endless questions, so knew to listen and not talk so much.

Father did try to explain before he left that it would all go well. He said it was complicated but that the United States was busy turning it into a territory. The Oregon Territory. I secretly wondered if that would really happen or were we moving to a new country?

But Father needed more land and he intended to do whatever it took to acquire more. It was becoming scarce and expensive in Virginia. He'd become well known as a good and fair horse trader, but it was difficult to make more than enough to just get by. The last straw was when Randy had been killed. He'd been his first-born and Jacob and I were sure he was his favorite. It had happened so suddenly and without reason. But that was what set him off. It was time he'd said, time for a new start. He was so upset but talked to no one that I knew of. Instead, he spent a good deal of time with the horses. Maybe they understood him.

But here we were - only where was Father? Would we ever see him again?

I was still brooding the next day when Uncle David came up looking like he had something on his mind and sure enough, "Maddie, you need to talk sense into Isabelle," he said.

"How'm I going to talk sense to her? She barely listens to me," except when I make a mistake, but I didn't say that out loud.

"She's not well and seems to be getting worse and she needs to stay here to get herself back together."

"What would I say to her that would make her listen?" I asked.

"Well, you can try that you're supposed to be waiting for your father."

"She wants to go on; she wants to get to Oregon. She's said that you and Uncle David will get us there."

"But Maddie, she's not doing so well; and we have a long road ahead of us."

"Are you going ahead?" I asked.

"Yup, we're contracted with this train and

now we've picked up ten or twelve more wagons. Your father gave us instructions that if the trip was too much for anyone to wait here and he'd be back to help."

"But now we don't know if he's coming."

"That's a fact," he said, his eyes not meeting mine. Guess he didn't feel that he needed to point out how careless I'd been with the letter. "I'll go talk with her again," he said.

But it did no good. Isabelle for reasons only she knew, was going to Oregon. Our four days in Independence were up. It was time to move on. We had made good time so far and other than a few rainstorms, the weather had held.

For whatever reason, I later thought she probably knew what was going to happen.

SEVEN

We weren't two days out of Independence when she died.

The wagon had shaken the entire night with her hacking cough. Hannah had slipped out before daybreak and had crawled in next to me as quiet as a mouse. It wasn't often that she left the safety of the wagon.

Maybe Isabelle had told her to leave.

Maybe Isabelle knew.

The coughing had stopped suddenly and I was able to sleep.

I'd overslept. Abigail Cantrell woke me with that syrupy voice of hers and the smell of fresh brewed coffee. "Would y'all care for a cup?" She did that now and again, maybe just to prove she was so much better at everything then I was.

Oh Lord, I thought what sort of day was this going to be. Why can't I just curl up and go back to sleep and pretend none of this was happening.

Dragging myself out from under the wagon, I

climbed over the back – I was quick so Isabelle couldn't tell me how unladylike I was behaving. And there she was. I looked at her face staring up at me, the eyes blank. They saw nothing. She wouldn't be telling me anything again - ever. I looked at her more closely. I guess I hadn't realized, she had actually been pretty. She looked much like I had pictured my real mother.

Isabelle's hair had thinned considerably over time and now there was a dried trickle of pink drool at the corner of her mouth. I had to do something but wasn't sure what. I could hear the Uncles talking over at the Cantrell's fire pit. I climbed down out of the wagon. My feet dragged and I guess I forgot I wasn't dressed decent when I went over to get them.

Guess they knew when they saw me. They both put their arms around me; I'd grown some and was nearly as tall as they were. Tears were threatening, burning behind my eyelids, but I was determined to hold back. There was a floodgate that wanted to open up and I was afraid to start, afraid what might happen.

They went into the wagon and then went to get Annie Runyon and her only surviving spinster sister. They'd take care of things. Why does everyone look for a spinster when a body has to be laid out?

Uncle Bert held up the wagon train 'til noon. There was an unspoken rule that we buried our dead and moved on, no matter who it was. Seems we'd be stopping too often. We'd never get anywhere if we didn't keep moving.

I gave the Runyon sisters Isabelle's best dress and one of our flannel sheets to wrap her in. Hannah clung to my hand as they lowered her into the fresh dug hole. Isabelle was the only mother she had ever known. Her eyes were boring into me looking for an explanation and then suddenly she hid behind me when she saw Rafferty Jones ride up. His one good eye stared down at us.

The two Uncles lowered her into the grave. It was shallow but what could we do? There didn't seem to be the time to have a proper burial, there were too many of them.

The men that had dug the hole hung around 'til we walked off, but we could hear the thump as each shovelful of dirt landed on that wrapped sheet. It jarred me to the very core. Jacob spent some time driving the supply wagon back and forth over the grave. Somehow tamping it down like that made it more secure. There were wolves in the area.

There was a numbness that had crept into me. I tried to think of what to do next, but I seemed to be stuck to the seat of the wagon. Hannah was by my side with her face under my apron barely breathing. She hadn't cried, but her little shoulders were slumped and she wouldn't look at me.

My eyes were glued to the horizon, not the one ahead but the one behind. I'm sure I was supposed to be doing something. I just couldn't figure what it was.

The Uncles came up to me and asked if I was OK to drive. I must have nodded my head because the reins were in my hands and we were moving. The rest of the day was a blur. We got to where we were going, but I hardly noticed. Hannah needed to be cared for, but I wasn't sure just what I should do for her. Miz Barnes walked back to get us and brought us to their fire for dinner. Jacob came too. The Barnes's served a fair meal of hash and beans. Other than that, they pretty much left us alone and didn't make us talk or anything. There were no words anyhow.

When I tucked Hannah in I crawled in next to her. I'd always slept under the wagon unless it was pouring down rain, but now I wasn't sure what to do with Hannah. She didn't want to sleep alone and I didn't want to sleep where you could almost still feel the warmth from the person we'd just buried. Hannah looked up at me, her eyes pleading with me to stay. I crawled in and closed my eyes. She cuddled up about as close as you can get to a person. We both fell into a sound sleep.

The next day we were up early and on the trail heading west as the sun peeked over the horizon. Uncle David pulled up next to our wagon and hopped up onto the seat. "Move over there, Miss Hannah Bell and make room for your favorite Uncle." Hannah gave him her cheeriest smile.

"Alright then Maddie, we need to talk." There were frown lines between his brows as he took the reins from my hands. "Gid-yup," he said to the oxen flicking the reins lightly. It wasn't necessary, they were so used to the trail they needed little direction.

A chill ran up and down my spine as I watched him pause, chewing over his thoughts. He hadn't ever ridden with us in the wagon. "I'm thinking maybe we could turn this rig around to let you all stay for a spell in Independence. You liked the town well enough," he said.

"What? How could you do that?" Even Hannah sat at attention.

"Well now hold on Maddie, 'fore you go gettin' all in a tizzy."

"I'm not in a tizzy. How can you think to leave us?"

"We won't be leaving you exactly," he said.

"Maybe just parting, temporary like." He flicked the reins again. Banger, our old lead ox half turned his head as though to ask, "What's up?"

"Now hear me out. If we let you three stay in Independence you can wait it out 'til your Pap comes to get you. More'n likely it won't be all that long. He was hoping to meet up with us mid-July so it won't be long." He cleared his throat and looked over at me. 'Bert and I have to go on with the train and it's not going to be easy with three additional children."

"I'm hardly a child." The words flew out of my mouth before I could stop them. "I'm fifteen. Why there are girls at home already married at fifteen. Why Daisy McGiver had her first young one by then."

"Now, now. I didn't mean to get you all riled up. I just don't know how we can do this. I'm not so sure your Pap would want us taking his children across the prairies and mountains without Isabelle to care for you."

Words failed me as I stared at him. Who had been cooking the meals, driving the wagon, gathering the wood, hauling water, milking Old Betsy and caring for Hannah all this time?

"And do you really consider Jacob a child?" I asked, trying not to sound so bitter. "He does more work than most men. Why he ..." But he cut me off.

"All right, all right," he said, the crinkles coming back to the corners of his eyes, "If you think you can do it, we'll give it a try. Don't know what Bert's gonna say or your Pap when we meet up with him, but I'll see what I can do."

The reins were back in my hands. I brought Hannah closer; I sat up straighter. "Hannah crawl in the wagon, see if you can find my bonnet." We were on our way to Oregon.

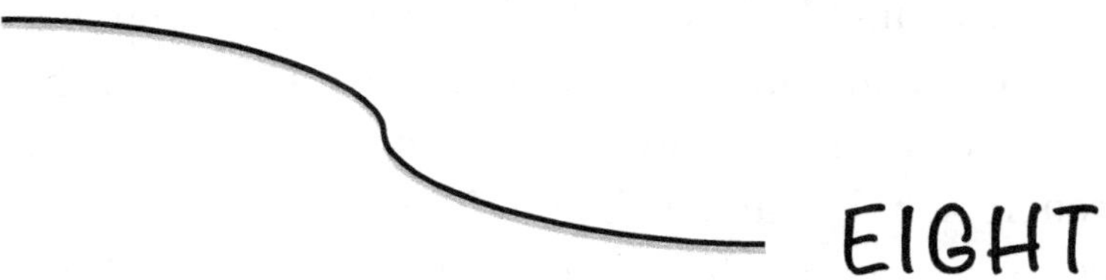

EIGHT

There were nearly twenty wagons in our caravan, plus the additional supply wagons. I guess you could see us coming with all the dust we raised. Uncle Bert tried to get us to spread out some and not bunch up so much together, which often happened. If one wagon towards the front slowed, then we all slowed. We were a long train, one after another snaking along the trail. It wasn't the best plan. All we did was take in each other's dust. But then we would be coming into open plains soon enough. Then we could all spread out and set our own pace.

But for now, we circled up early; everyone was just plain old tuckered out. I let Hannah go off and collect berries with the other children. I poked around trying to find something different to put into the pot for tonight's dinner. It hadn't been more than 15 minutes when someone yelled "Indians." The spoon flew from my hands, I nearly knocked the stew pot over and I'm sure my feet didn't touch the ground as I ran outside the circle.

"Hannah!" I screeched. I searched one way and then the other. I could just see the top of her bonnet in the distance. It took only seconds to reach her. I grabbed her before she even saw me coming and dashed back into the circle. She'd grown some, but still felt light as a feather. She clung to that basket, so proud of what she'd gathered by herself.

"Stay down," I said and I wasn't any too gentle pushing her into the wagon. This was Arapaho country. Uncle David said they could be none too pleasant and we needed to keep a careful eye out. As I was pulling the rifle out from under the wagon seat, Uncle Bert yelled out, "It's OK." We watched in disbelief as twenty or so dark bronze, nearly naked Indians, walked into the circle. Two of the largest, their bodies shiny with bear grease, their long black hair hanging in some sort of braids fashioned with a red fabric, came over to my campfire. They sat themselves down on a log. My heart was in my throat. I slipped the rifle back under the wagon seat, still within easy reach.

Uncle David came over; "Feed them," he said, "Think they're Arapaho." Like that was going to make a difference as to who they were. Truth be known, I wasn't any too comfortable being around any of them. And the fact that there were three dried up scalps hanging from the thong tied around the taller one's waist, wasn't going to make for a restful dinner.

"Doesn't seem like they're looking for trouble," said Uncle David, "just a hot meal and maybe they're just curious about who's taking over their lands."

"We're not homesteading here," I said.

"I know that, but they don't and they're gettin' kinda sick of our coming through their land; shooting all their buffalo and trapping all their beaver. Their tempers are running a bit short so let's just feed 'em and hope for the best."

My hands shook as I spooned up two bowls of the venison stew. Well, it was almost venison stew. There had been one very small piece left from the deer that Mr. Barnes had shot and shared a while back. But those Indians didn't seem to mind. They didn't take a breath while they inhaled that stew. Maybe my cooking was getting better. They passed the empty bowls back and grunted. "They want more," said Uncle David.

"Really," I said, not meaning to be quite as sassy as it sounded. When they were through, they'd each consumed four bowls of stew! That would be our entire dinner. Without a by-your-leave the entire band got up and stalked off, scalps swinging from the hips of some of them.

"Look at it this way," said Uncle Bert. "We still have our hair."

We made do with cold cornbread for dinner and a few leftover beans.

The incident would have been forgotten except during the night they must have returned. In the morning we were missing at least a dozen horses, three of them had been from Father's herd.

"Well that was a fine thank you," said Uncle Bert. "No sense tracking them," he said. "Seems they headed downstream. It'd take days to catch up with them. If that's our only loss we're doing just fine."

As he spoke I watched as dark clouds began to gather in the west. "Let's get a move on," he said. "Get some miles behind us 'fore that storm breaks. All up," he yelled. First one way then the other.

We made some progress before that storm met us and it looked like it meant business. Uncle Bert had us hunker down in a tight circle. The wranglers drove the cattle inside; the last thing we were going to need was a stampede. Once inside the circle of wagons they generally stayed fairly calm.

That storm had been creeping up on us for a few hours when it broke open with a fury that made my hair stand on end. The sky was green before the clouds actually got over us. Then it turned black. So close to nighttime black that I'd forgotten it was only lunchtime. The wind, the roar, and the lightning were enough to scare the starch right out of you.

I climbed in the wagon with Hannah and tried to put a pillow round her head to block out some of the noise. I'll tell you there was some fright in her eyes, but she wasn't the only one! The crashing from the lightning – then followed by the boom of thunder –I was quite sure the world was coming to an end.

The cattle were moaning and getting restless. You could hear them stomping around and even pushing against the wagons. They were packed in so tight; there was little room for them to wander. Between their bawling and the uproar with the booming of thunder and the bright flashes streaking across the sky, I wasn't sure if any of us would ever see tomorrow.

There was a tremendous crack of lightning so close; I could smell the burned air. That was it. That was more than the oxen and horses could take.

Whichever was leading, and we never did find out which group it was, the horses or oxen or cows or the few mules we had, they all started to bawl. In a panic, they pushed against one of the wagons 'til they had pushed it over. The screams went through the camp and then a few of the animals pushed through near the toppled wagon and were gone. The men grabbed at the rest and turned them back. The Uncles were riding bareback on two horses I'd never seen before.

There was a sudden downburst of rain that lasted seconds only. But it blew so hard it felt as if our wagon was going to go flying through the air. Was this what a tornado was I wondered.

And then - it stopped as fast as it had started; it was as if it had never even rained. There was a great commotion outside with everyone scurrying about trying to help the family in the tipped over wagon. It was one of the new families we'd picked up in Independence. It was a group where none of them spoke any English. They'd seemed nice enough. They were mostly blond and there were lots of kids. No one could understand a word they'd said.

"Maddie, where's Hannah?" asked Jacob.

"She's alright; she's back in the wagon."

"Hitch up," yelled Uncle David. "Quick everyone. Do it now." He was yelling, trying to be heard over the panic that had spread thru the train.

With Jacob yanking and pulling our oxen, I tried my best to get them yoked.

"Get moving," yelled Uncle Bert. "Quick now." He was still astride his horse. "Move it. Get up there Maddie, and get that wagon turned around. Move."

I couldn't imagine what he was talking about and wanted to question him when the choking smell of smoke almost gagged me. The oxen, their eyes nearly bulging out of their heads didn't need any urging.

Maneuvering around in the tight space was not easy but seeing the orange flames licking at the prairie grasses and turning the world black hastened our retreat. The wagon turned just as the grass beneath the wheels caught. The oxen, close to panic, moved faster than they even knew they could. Banger, our old ox was pulling for all he was worth. The yoke was not fastened properly threatening to break apart.

We made for the stream that we'd so recently camped next to. Yelling and whipping them harder than I'd intended I drove them into the sloshing water. They were up to their shoulders. I yanked on the reins for them to stop. The burning embers were raining down on us, the canvas threatening to catch fire.

"Hannah, get out here." Taking a quilt, I soaked it in the river ready to wrap it around her. The fire came up to the river's edge. The burning, searing heat was so hot it was threatening to scorch us. The oxen bawled. I couldn't take them out of the yoke or we'd lose them for sure. Other wagons were joining us; some had huge burn holes in their canvas tops.

There was bedlam, one wagon tipped over; the oxen too scared to stop kept dragging it further down the river.

"Hannah come out here," I yelled again. There was no answer.

Some people were running ahead of the flames having left their wagons. A young boy was running towards me, his clothes on fire. I jumped down and half swam and half ran through the river coming out trailing a huge stream of water. Running towards him, I scooped him up and ran into the water with him. The flames scorched my hands and I listened to the sizzle as the water quenched the burning flesh on his back. The stench was nearly gagging. The boy moaned, I looked down; it was Sean Patrick, Brian's younger brother. I held him close to me and said words I didn't even know.

Brian pushed through the water, "I'll take him Maddie." I handed him over and swiped at the tears dripping from my chin. How could this be?

But where was Hannah? I waded back to the wagon and pulled it apart, looking everywhere. She wasn't there. Uncle Bert, astride his horse, paced up and down along the stream looking and watching and counting.

"Hannah, I can't find Hannah," I screamed. Uncle Bert wheeled his horse around and galloped back to where we had come from, through the flames. The horse kicked up the ashes and burning embers from the grass. His hooves must have been about scorched through.

Wading through the water I went from one wagon to the next asking one after another if they'd seen Hannah. I'd nearly given up, tears and soot and water blinded my eyes just as Mr. Barnes, his horse kicking up a spray of water galloped towards me.

He handed Hannah down to me. She had been sitting up atop his horse her face buried in his shirt. So much was going on. "She'd been hiding in the back of our wagon," he said and galloped off.

Holding her close and whispering words that only she could hear, I waded back to our wagon; the oxen were bellowing their displeasure at having been left in the middle of the stream.

Settling Hannah next to me with a stern warning, I got the animals moving back across the stream to where the grass was still green and untouched. We didn't want to look where we had just been. It was a field of black ash. There was nothing left. The few trees that had been there were smoldering black stumps. It looked like there was an outline of a tipped over wagon, but it was hard to see between the wisps of smoke rising from the scorched earth.

"Lightning," said one of the men. "Not much you can do about it. Get one of them prairie fires going and it takes all hell and damnation to put it out." He spat into the dirt. "God knows where we'd all be right now if we didn't have the stream." I didn't want to think about it. I made myself busy shaking out the quilts and sheets that had soot and ash all over them.

Uncle Bert didn't come back.

I had pulled together a meal of sorts. Seems like no one wanted to start a fire, we were all pretty content with another meal of cold beans, bacon and cornbread. Most of the men had been riding back and forth, to where the storm had struck. I heard talk that only a little two-year-old girl survived in the wagon that had been tipped over in the panic. Uncle Bert had brought her as far as the river and one of the other wagons had picked her up. He had then gone back and forth leading other wagons through the burning prairie. Many hadn't been sure which way to go. Uncle David said he'd told him that Hannah had been found, but still Uncle Bert went back to be sure they all had made it to the stream. He didn't come to dinner.

I was making myself busy with trying to brush the soot out of the wagon and fussing over Hannah when Uncle David unsaddled his horse and put the shovel back up. He made himself comfortable before he started to talk.

"He helped that little blonde girl, had to pry her fingers off her mother. She didn't understand one word of English." He took his hat off and wiped his forehead. "The flames were already eating at the top of the wagon what with it fallen over and all."

Why wasn't he telling me about Uncle Bert? "Seems there were three other little ones in that wagon but when it went over everything in it fell on them. The mother was thrown clear but those panicked animals didn't allow for her to get out of the way."

He drew on his unlit pipe, not even noticing that it wasn't lit, he cradled it with fingers raw from burns. "The father came up on his horse and tried to get to the mother and they were knocked down, man and horse..." He shook his head. A tear, unnoticed, slipped down making a crazy pattern on his soot-covered cheek. What about Uncle Bert I wanted to scream?

"Lost some cattle, but I guess we can make it up. No sense crying over spilt milk." I held Hannah closer on my lap, pulling her face into my neck. I watched as Uncle David continued to toy with his pipe, then ran his fingers through his scorched beard. Quiet, I thought to myself. You don't need to fill every moment with chatter.

"He was my twin you know. Don't think we've been separated for more'n a day since the day we was born." He puffed on his pipe again, his cheeks drawing in.

"It was his horse. Now and again they get spooked. You know that. Bert was some good with horses, I'll tell you, but this one was just plain out spooked. With the fire and heat and the animals not knowing what to do, and the lightning, his horse was just plain out crazed.

"He took off for God knows where. He tripped. More'n likely a prairie dog hole He went down taking Bert with him. Broke his neck he did. A fall like that will kill a person no matter how tough. He was dead soon's he hit the ground."

He sucked again on the unlit pipe, his eyes staring into the distance. "Had to shoot that horse – not that he was that badly injured mind you. But had to shoot him anyways. Shot him through the head, his leg looked broke, didn't bother looking too close, but his time had come."

He rose up, knocked the ashes that weren't there out of his pipe and tucked it back in his pocket. "Well Bert's gone and there's nothing a body can do about it."

That was as much as Uncle David was ever going to say. That was the end of the story. I held Hannah a long time and just rocked her back and forth. The wagon train was very quiet all night. It seemed even the babies knew not to cry out.

In the morning when I went out to untether the oxen, Banger was dead. He just laid there on his side. It had been too much for his old body. Between the fire and the river crossings and the lightning and the weight of the wagon, he'd done more than his share.

I tried to get him up. I didn't subscribe to hitting animals, but I hit that ox. I have no idea what got into me, but I punched him with my fist. I yelled at him, "Get up you ox, get up."

My foot felt like I'd gone and broke it I kicked him so hard, but I still yelled. "Get up you lazy no good ox. Get up." I took a stick and started to hit him on the head. His eye was blank, it just stared and stared up to the sky. His sides were not moving. There was no life there. There was nothing to get up and still I yelled.

"Get up you no account, no good ox." Uncle David came up behind me. He slipped his arms around me and kept saying over and over, "It's alright now, it's alright. Go easy, It's alright."

When there was no fight left, when I was sure I'd never walk again 'cause I'd kicked that ox so many times, I started to cry. Uncle David just held me and told me over and over "It's going to be alright. It's going to be alright." I'm too big to hold on anyone's lap but he set himself down on a log and held me there 'til the sobs tapered off and I was quiet.

It was just the next day when I met Gabriella.

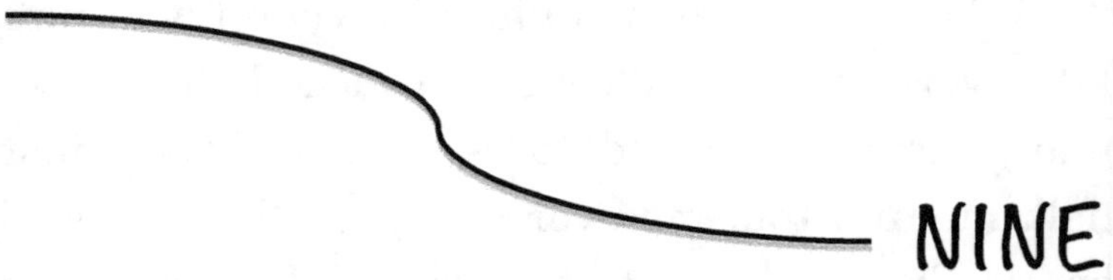

NINE

It was later than usual when we were all hitched up and ready for travel. Seemed no one's heart was in it, but we had to push forward. Uncle David became the unofficial leader; no one else seemed to have much interest in doing it. He rallied all of us and we managed to form a somewhat haphazard line. He rode us hard. It was our first day out with just him leading. I think he wanted us to be so exhausted that when we pulled over for the night we'd all sleep soundly. I think he wanted to be as far away as possible from the smell of burned grass and all that went with it.

Near sunset, after we circled up, I went to do my business in the woods. I was carrying my rifle. Uncle David had said now that we were coming into a different area you couldn't always tell about the Indians round these parts.

Isabelle was no longer with us to disapprove of my carrying a rifle.

When there were trees in the area, the women

would often go off by themselves, or with someone else, for a moment to tend to their bodily functions as Isabelle had called it. I left Hannah in the wagon happily playing with her doll and went off. I didn't need to go too far into the woods, it was pretty dark and tangled so I was only a few feet in when I heard a noise. My heart stopped, I hadn't been watching where I was going, I was sure I was going to meet a whole tribe of Indians.

I heard the noise again, sorta like "psssst" only very low, almost like the breath of wind through the treetops. My eyes hadn't quite adjusted to the darkness as I searched around for the noise. And there stood a girl. She looked to be about my age. She was standing stock still, her eyes shifting between me and the dark ball of fur rooting around in the underbrush. I knew what it was. I think I'd rather it was a tribe of Indians!

The girl stuck a foot out behind her and took one silent step back. She knew she had my attention so kept her eyes on the black coat of fur meandering about in search of food. As innocent as it looked, it was anything but. We heard more than our fair share of stories from the men as to the ferociousness of the grizzly bear. This one so far had not seen us, hadn't smelled us either as the wind was going the other way. He was not particularly big, but grizzlies were fast and uncommonly angry most of the time.

The girl continued to step back. She had a basket over her arm that was half filled with berries. Grizzlies love berries. The sound of a breaking stick pierced the silence. She froze. The bear's head was up, his nose sniffing the air, one-way and then another. His body tensed a moment.

"Drop the basket," I whispered. She didn't hear me. "Drop the basket."

If you can yell a whisper, that's what I did. The bear rose up. I think my mouth must have dropped open as he rose to his full height. The girl let her basket fall, probably not intentionally. This was not a baby bear.

With grizzlies, I've been told their eyesight isn't so good, but they have a keen sense of smell and this one's nose was twitching to beat all. We weren't thirty feet from that massive hulk. And talk about smell! He stunk. He lowered himself from his standing position, let out a low rumbling warning growl.

I do not know how I got that gun up to my shoulder and got a shot off before he started in our direction but the bang of that shot scared me about as much as it scared anyone.

I shot. We ran. We heard him roaring a scream

and crashing through the bushes right behind us but the shot took effect, not quite as quickly as I'd have liked.

I think I saw my life pass before my eyes, as I was sure I was going to die. It took a minute, but the shot had reached its mark. That bear never even broke through the tree line. We heard a tremendous crash.

We ran so fast and were yelling louder than I knew was possible. They saw us coming. Or heard us maybe. Heard us is more like the truth. Men and guns met us as the girl yelled, "Bear." My words were stuck solid in my throat, I don't think there was a squeak left in me. We ran inside the circle, our sides heaving.

For whatever senseless reason, we took one look at each other and smiled. Before we knew what was happening, we laughed. We couldn't help it. We laughed ourselves sick. I have no idea why. One minute we were almost dead, the next we're falling over with laughter.

Jacob came up to tell us he didn't think it was funny at all. He said that the bear was almost six feet tall and we could've been killed. His annoyance only made us laugh harder. We laughed 'til tears ran down our cheeks. We only stopped when our sides hurt so much we almost couldn't breathe.

When we could catch our breath, she said her name was Gabriella. That made me laugh even more 'cause who'd ever heard of anyone named Gabriella. She laughed too. She had olive skin, black straight hair and was the kind of pretty that I'd always wished I could be. She said she was Spanish. I'd never met a Spanish girl before but I liked her well enough.

She asked my name and I said "Madison." Jacob, of course, was standing there and had to add his two bits worth and said, "Whoever heard of a girl named Madison? That's a president's name, not a girl's name." He acted like that was the first time he'd ever heard it. Well, we could not help it - it started us off again. Jacob just stood there looking at us like we were a couple of fools.

When I could get control of myself, I told her that was my brother and she could ignore him. Then I asked her where did she come from and how did she happen to be on this wagon train.

"I came on in St. Louis," she said. "But we didn't hitch up with your group 'til Independence. We came up the Mississippi by riverboat. My parents died, so I'm with the Henderson's. We will go to Oregon Country. It was my parent's dream." She had an accent but it was nice enough.

"Are the Henderson's your family?"

"No, I have no family here, they are all down in the Mexico area."

"Do you want to go back then?" I was still having trouble catching my breath, but I wanted to know who I'd nearly been killed with.

"Si, but I cannot. I have no way to get back there. I have no money."

I was still thinking about "Si" when I realized it was Spanish for Yes. Then I was thinking of a hundred other questions when a voice cut our conversation in two, "Gabriella where are you?" A tall, angular woman, her face sharp, came up to us. "Gabriella, must I always come searching for you?"

"No," she said and hung her head, her hands folded themselves over her apron.

"And where pray tell is the basket and the berries that I sent you for?"

"Lost," she said.

"How can you be so careless?" If she only knew, I thought! She gave Gabriella a push in the direction of their wagon. Jacob and Hannah were standing just behind me - Miz Henderson never even said hello or a by-your-leave or anything.

"Looks like your new friend isn't going to be real happy this trip," said Jacob.

"Oh Jacob, you don't know everything."

But he did. Gabriella had become the Henderson's slave. We would meet by the stream when we were drawing water, or out on the trail when we were in search of buffalo chips for our fires, and then we'd get to talk. Sometimes if the Henderson's turned in early, she would come down to my campfire and we could sit and talk. The Henderson's had one sickly baby that Gabriella was in charge of, that as well as doing all the chores that they had given her to do.

That baby was up most nights crying and Gabriella was responsible for her. Some nights she brought her down by our fire. That little baby looked like it was about starved. She had blue circles under her eyes and her little cheekbones kind of poked out of her skin. I gave Gabriella whatever milk we had from Old Betsy but I'm not so sure that agreed with her. She threw up most of whatever Gabriella fed her but she seemed to like our voices whispering next to the fire at night. It seemed to quiet her some to be with us.

"My father, he was from Mexico, my mother, she was from the Texas area, down by the Rio Grande. They tried to settle near the border to raise horses, but it was not good. There are many problems there so they decide to go to Oregon Country."

"My father raises horses, too," I said, "Maybe you can stay with us in Oregon."

"Maybe," she said, "If the Henderson's let me go." The baby was becoming fretful again, so Gabriella rose up and walked about trying to calm her.

"And where is your family?" she asked.

Where to start I thought. Do we have all night?

"My father is on his way to meet us. I hope." I poked at the fire with a long stick releasing a spray of sparks. "My real mother died before I ever really knew her. She'd been sick a real long time and when she had Hannah she died. I had a brother named Randy. He was older than me. He was killed by horse thieves. We think. We don't know exactly who or exactly what happened. Then my stepmother Isabelle died a few weeks ago on the trail." There was a catch in my throat and the words stopped coming.

"I'm sorry," she said. "Sorry for so many troubles."

"Well, it's alright, actually. I guess I really miss my brother Randy and my father the most."

"You would miss your brother more than your mother?" she asked.

"Randy took care of me since I was very little.

Since my mother was always sick. Yes, I miss him most, I guess. I just wonder always, what happened to him? Maybe we'll never know."

"And what of your other brother, Jacob."

"Well, he's more of a pest than anything else. He just wants to aggravate everyone." This made Gabriella laugh which woke the baby. Now she'd be up half the night trying to get her back to sleep. I took a turn and walked back and forth with her for a while but I was tired too. I spent most days driving the wagon. Gabriella spent most days in the back of the Henderson's wagon where she could snooze with the baby. The Henderson's did not like her visiting with me. I'm not sure why. I guess we just had too much fun.

TEN

Cholera! Yes, I'd heard of it, but it wasn't that common back in Virginia. I remember when the Wilson family had it but they were quarantined so fast that it never got much beyond their farm. Course they did lose all but James, their middle son.

Sometimes when I think of the graves I left behind, I just have to remember about the Wilson's losses. James and his father were all that was left of seven children, a mother, grandmother and most of their slaves got it too. The Wilsons never did recover from their loss. Mr. Wilson and James ended up selling the farm and going back east.

Gabriella had asked about it. Did I have any magic cure? I told her what Sadie's mother had said: "You think someone you know has it, get as far away from them as you can, and boil the water. Boil any water that you plan to drink."

Well darned if the Barnes's wagon didn't

seem to have it and then before you knew what happened it'd traveled through six other wagons. For whatever reason, the Cantrell wagon wasn't touched. Abigail and her young brother seemed fine, even her father, a snarly old man, didn't seem to be bothered at all. I wasn't friends with Abigail Cantrell, but wondered sometimes why she put up with her father's nastiness.

"She's got it." Gabriella held out the Henderson's baby. Odd, I didn't even know her name. Gabriella always called her bebé, which was Spanish. Maybe we didn't want her to have a name. On this night, Gabriella sat by the fire trying to soothe the fretful little one.

"Maddie, I don't know what else to do for her, she is so sick." Gabriella's tears dripped off the sides of her chin onto the tiny bundle. Maybe they would cool the hot little body. "Her parents, they are so sick. I have given them everything I can think of, nothing will cure it."

"We have no medicine except laudanum and that won't do it," I said. I didn't want to tell her again what Sadie's mother had said about staying away from people sick with the cholera. "We can put a bit of crushed onion in her bottle. I know Sadie's mother had done that for some stomach complaints."

"My parents died of this while we came up the Mississippi from New Orleans," she said. "It happened so fast. One day they were fine, the next day my father, he died. The next day my mother, she died too."

"What did they give them? Wasn't there something they could do?"

"There was nothing. They try the bleeding and leeches, it made them worse."

But then, for reasons we couldn't understand, the baby survived. Seven others on the wagon train did not. For the next week of travel, there was a new grave left behind each day. The parents of the baby, Mr. and Mrs. Henderson, died within hours of each other. Four men died and one of the McElhinney boys. Brian had come up alongside my wagon one sweltering day to tell me.

"Joseph has it," he said, "Don't think he'll make it 'til nightfall."

"I'm sorry Brian." Joseph was his favorite brother.

"I meant to thank you," he said, "for helping Sean Patrick after he came through that fire." Maybe having Joseph so sick made him think back to how he'd almost lost another brother.

My tongue was tied. I tried to think of something more to say and wished I had Isabelle's

good sense of conversation and could say something that sounded right. I was quite sure Joseph
wasn't going to make it. I sat there my mind
abuzz but nothing would come.

No matter if I could think to say something or
not, Sean Patrick had not died. That was a good
thing. His burns from that dreadful prairie fire
were so severe there was not one reason why he
should have survived, but he did. He would probably have scars forever, but he was alive. Brian
had said it was because I'd dunked him in the water so quickly and put out the flames that were
burning him.

All I could think to say was "Is your mother
well?" Maybe that was about as much as anyone
could say.

"Well enough," he answered. I had the feeling
he wanted to talk more; but he, too, was at a loss.
We seemed to have an awful lot of dead people
between us.

There were now nearly two dozen wagons
with a few stragglers that had joined us. The
stragglers were families that had been separated
from their original wagon trains for one reason or
another. Often the wagons had problems and
weren't able to continue and had to spend time in
Independence. One who Jacob had spoken with

had to hold back because of sickness. Another, because the wagon needed so many repairs it could not go on. That one had to replace or repair nearly everything, including all four wheels. This could be very expensive and the delay could be dangerous as wagons leaving late for the trek across the prairie and the mountains could become deadly. It was near impossible to get through if they didn't stay ahead of the winter.We had all mostly tried to do our own repairs, but there were times when it couldn't be done. Independence seemed to have an abundance of wagon fixing places, so if you had to break down, that certainly was the place to do it.

Course from what I saw, the wagon trains weren't too anxious to wait for anyone who was going to be delayed for too long with repairs or any other reason. It didn't seem to be much of a problem though as anyone who was held up could join any of the other groups coming through. Most didn't mind who or how many connected with them. Most felt the more the better. Nearly all of the wagon trains that we met up with had all had considerable loss along the trail, not only possessions and livestock but too often accidents or illness. Additional wagons were welcomed.

Some coming from the east actually turned

back after getting all this way. Hard to imagine, but there were those who just plain ran out of provisions and money and maybe gumption and had no choice but to turn around and head back. We passed a few of those. I didn't see anyone who looked any too happy with that decision. Most that we'd seen were women. Didn't see too many boys or men. A sorry affair to be sure.

And now, from a wagon that had joined us in Independence, I'd met Gabriella. She was fast becoming my best friend, I guess maybe my only friend. It was nice seeing someone my age at night, even though we were both now caring for young ones. I had Hannah, she had Sara. Gabriella said the baby's real name was Henrietta Maude Henderson, but that was too big a name for one so tiny. She named her Sara, just plain Sara. Nights, after we'd circle up and get the wagons settled down, we would share a campfire.

"Never saw Jacob work so hard," I said as he laid out our evening fire.

"He is good to help. What would we do if he weren't here," she said.

"I'm thinking he's sweet on you Gabriella," I said. "Jacob does nothing unless there's a little something in it for him."

"He can be sweet on me if he likes," she answered, "We've got a long way to go and I could not manage the wagon and the baby and the animals alone." She sounded a mite short with me so I moved on to safer ground.

"Uncle David said that tomorrow we'll be at the halfway point. Well halfway from Missouri anyhow. He said we just may get there by October." October I groaned inwardly, he may as well have said next year it was so far away.

"We need to celebrate," said Gabriella, "Your Uncle said we'd be traveling over the Continental Divide next week and I think that would be a good time to have a celebration. Surely, there's someone on this wagon train that can play a fiddle or dance a jig?"

Sure enough, everyone thought it was a grand idea and all wanted to be part of our first ever party. Two of the wranglers played a fiddle and one of the young boys played a Jews harp. The wrangler with the fiddle couldn't keep his feet still and danced atop the tailgate of the wagon, making a wonderful racket with the clatter of boot heels on the wooden slats. We clapped and we sang. Even Gabriella's baby, Sara, seemed to perk up a bit.

Jacob came over and asked her to dance, she

had a good two years on him, but neither one seemed to mind at all. I tapped my foot and bounced Hannah and swung her around a few times when Brian came over.

"Mind if I join you two?" I wondered where Abigail Cantrell was.

"Sure," I said, laughing at Hannah's imitation of a dance. Brian picked up Hannah and put his arm around my waist as he swung us around. I was too shy to meet his eyes, but I sure did like his arm around me. He swung me around into the shadows between two of the wagons. He stopped. He was still holding Hannah in one arm. I looked up at him to see why we weren't dancing.

My heart nearly stopped. From the light of the fire, I could see the blueness of his eyes looking into me. This was a new feeling I'd never had before. His arm was still around my waist as he leaned down.

"Indians!" There were screams. The music stopped. Brian shoved Hannah at me, "Get to your wagon." He dashed for his gun. I ran to our wagon and grabbed my gun.

"Hannah, you stay down." I pushed her into the wagon between the bureau and the blanket chest. The Indians were coming at us from all directions. The war whoops filled the air. It was so dark we couldn't see very well and couldn't take aim until they were almost on top of us. I used a barrel at the back of the wagon for cover as I shot first in one direction and then another. From early on, both Uncles had assured us that most of the Indians were friendly and only wanted to trade. This did not look like a group wanting anything less than our scalps.

There were screams from both sides. They'd gotten inside our protected circle, whooping and yelling. Listening to the hullabaloo it made me angry. I took foolish chances, rising up from behind the barrel to get a good aim, then ducking back down again to reload.

There was gunfire everywhere and arrows flying through the air, some meeting their mark. Some of the arrows were lit with fire and aimed at the canvas tops. Two of the wagons had their covers ablaze. Then it happened: I turned back to take aim and looked up to see what would be my worst ever nightmare.

An Indian, his hair stuck with raggedy feathers, his tomahawk raised over his head, was ready to take my scalp. There wasn't time even to take aim when I heard a shot. It was fired so close to my ear that the ringing didn't go away for hours. A spurt of blood came out from the hole in his head. He dropped that tomahawk, the one he was about to use to separate me from my hair.

His horse not knowing what happened, leaped up pawing the air, where was his master? The horse came down hard then galloped off dragging the dead weight that was tangled in the reins

"Move over." Abigail Cantrell, her voice steel like, elbowed me over.

"Wow," was all I could say. Most men can't get off a shot like that even after years of practice.

"Lucky shot," she said. "Here come some more."

There's no telling how long it kept up. And then it seemed that as fast as they came - suddenly they were gone. The noise of battle stopped. Then the moans began. There were bodies on both sides. I came down from my perch on the wagon's tailgate and looked around. Everything was a mess. Confusion was everywhere.

"So, Abigail..." I began. But she walked off cradling her rifle looking as if she'd been born with it tucked in her arms. I went in search of Jacob and to check on the others.

And if we hadn't enough, I saw Uncle David slumped against the wheel of our supply wagon. There was an arrow sticking out of his middle. By the looks of it, it hadn't gone all the way through. My heart wanted to stop beating.

Jacob got to him before I did and in a fit of anger yanked out the arrow. Blood spewed out covering his hands. My mind was having trouble with what I was seeing. There were bodies scattered about, some moaning, and some not moving at all. I got up into the wagon and grabbed Jacob's quilt. With great care, we eased him down to lie flat. I dashed back in for a flannel sheet and tore it into strips, pressing them to the wound that didn't want to stop oozing. Jacob went in search of water. This can't be my mind said over and over.

"Maddie, it's not good news. You know that girl, don't deny it." I looked down at the piece of flannel pressed against his middle. There was bright red blood seeping through. That wasn't a good color. I knew that much at least. It was fresh blood and it wasn't going to stop.

"Can I do something?" I asked, ashamed for having no idea what I should be doing for him.

"Not much you can do with a gut wound. Sit here awhile," he said. "I need to tell you a story." I sat on the log next to him and wrapped my arms around my knees. Why I wondered would he want to tell a story with the little time that remained.

He breathed for a while, trying to take in deep gulps of air but then wincing before letting it back out.

"Maddie, I knew yer' mother." I shook my head. I knew this.

"She was sick a long time. When she died your Pap was so upset. He felt it was his fault. If they hadn't had Hannah she wouldn't have died."

With this he rested a moment, his hand seeking out the wound. A quiet gasp escaped when his fingers met the warm sticky blood. His eyes closed. I leaned over to listen, to hear if he was still breathing. His eyes opened again. Easy enough to see - the life was slipping out of him.

"He never forgave himself. He went up north to tell her parents. They never did approve of your father, wanted your mother to marry someone from Boston."

His eyes were closed. I patted his hand to let him know I was still there. "Well, he met your mother's sister for the first time, she too had been ill," his voice was close to a whisper. "Fact was Doctors had told her she may not have more'n a few years at most." It was hard to hear what he was saying. I leaned closer. "Your father married her. He thought he could help her."

I sucked in my breath. What was he saying?

"You mean Isabelle?"

"That I would." He sighed.

"You mean Isabelle was my mother's sister?" My mind tried to accept this. "Why didn't Father tell me that? Why didn't Isabelle tell me?"

He waited a moment then said, "Maddie, she was dying from the time your father brought her home. She had something wrong with her lungs." He tried to focus his eyes on me. The blueness was becoming dim. "They didn't want you children to become attached to her after you'd already lost your own mother." His eyes closed a moment.

"There's more to tell," he said and sighed. "Just know that Isabelle loved you and wanted to help your father and help you and Jacob and Hannah." His voice was trailing off and I almost couldn't hear what else he said. "That was why she agreed to move to Virginia. She knew she wouldn't last that long."

He coughed a shallow, raspy sound; blood trickled down from the corner of his mouth, a trail running into his tangled beard. "She thought she could make it to Oregon, to get you there." He stopped. "There's more," this was more of a gasp than just words. "Randy, your brother, and Rafferty, the wrangler ..." His breathing stopped. His eyes stayed open. The blood from the wound stopped flowing. The words had ended. There was no more.

~

For the next three days we stayed circled up and we did what we had to. There were too many bodies to bury. There were too many bodies to try to heal. The cattle and horses were spread out far and wide. The sound of the shovels digging the holes was all that broke the silence.

We were probably still in some unnamed, unorganized territory on a flat endless plain. The last night there I sat next to the fire watching the embers die away as sparks drifted up into the night sky. And then out of nowhere, there was Rafferty Jones. I hadn't heard him and there he was, his hat pulled low, his one good eye staring at me. When I looked up at him he turned abruptly and disappeared into the shadows.

What I wondered did Uncle David mean by Randy and Rafferty? My brother? That brother was dead. And our wrangler?

ELEVEN

Would we ever get back on the trail? We'd spent so much time making repairs and burying our dead that it seemed like we'd be getting into the snow season if we didn't get moving. It was already the end of the summer. With the river crossings and the hold ups trying to corral our wandering cattle, we were now well behind schedule.

"By tomorrow we should reach the 'parting of the ways,'" said Jacob. "We'll need to make a decision."

"Well, what kind of decision?" I asked, wondering how he'd all of a sudden become boss.

He pushed his hat back. Without it shading his eyes, it showed how young he really was. "Which way to go. Look here," he said, spreading out a map. "If we take the northern route we'll cut out 80-90 miles, that's a week's worth of travel."

"And what about this route," I asked pointing to the map. "It goes down to Ft. Bridger, we could lay in more supplies."

"Yes we could," he said. "But we don't have all that much money left so there wouldn't be that many more supplies that we could buy."

"I'd rather go the short way," I answered.

"Well we're going to need to ask the others," he said. "There are so few left. Maybe we should take a head count tonight after dinner to see how many we are and what's in their minds."

I guess we hadn't realized how few there were left. There were still about twenty wagons. There were boys as young as eight driving some of the supply wagons and most all of the women and girls were now driving their own rigs.

There were only three men left from those who started out with us in Virginia: Mr. Barnes and Mr. Runyon and Jane Applegate's father. The Runyon's stayed even more to themselves after their spinster sister had drowned back at our first river crossing. Mr. Runyon was still about as cantankerous as always. It appeared his wife was going to have a little one sometime soon, but I didn't even want to think about that.

"So, how many want to take Sublette's Cutoff and how many are for going to Ft. Bridger?" asked Mr. Barnes. After a lot of talk most everyone agreed, it was getting late in the year, we needed to move quickly. "You all know that you won't be finding any water or food for the animals if we take that cut off."

"Suits us just fine," said Mr. Applegate. "We'll be taking plenty with us."

I noticed Abigail Cantrell standing in the shadows, not wanting to be part of the group. When it had all quieted down some I went over to her fire.

"That was a fine shot," I said, "I mean with that Indian and all. You're a good shot. Thank you." She didn't say anything so I said, "Real sorry about your father." I guess I was getting better at making polite conversation when there'd been a death. Not sure if that was something I really wanted to get good at. But her father had been one of the first that the Indians had gotten.

"Don't be sorry," she said, some of the drawl had returned, but somehow I didn't mind it so much now.

"My brother and I will do just fine." I wasn't sure what to say next so chose to keep quiet. Isabelle would've been proud of me, I was learning to think before I spoke.

"He deserved to die." Another opportunity to keep my silence, however, I'm quite sure my eyes showed my surprise at what she'd said.

I said, "Um." And poked at the fire.

Guess sometimes it's a whole lot better to listen than speak. This may have been one of those times.

"He wasn't good to me," she said. "My mother died because he wouldn't care for her properly and he was not good to us." Tears were coming into her eyes and she picked up a stick too. Together we poked at the fire and watched the sparks drift up and disappear into the blackness of the night.

Hard to remember all that she said, I guess maybe I'm not such a good listener, some words went right by me, especially the ones I didn't want to hear. She spoke quietly and there were parts that I missed. She had her handkerchief out and it was pretty well soaked by the time we parted. I used my sleeve mostly. It was pretty close to midnight when she'd talked herself out. I got up to leave. She whispered, "Thank you."

I said something like, "Sometime maybe you could show me how to make that coffee that everyone likes so much."

The next day we picked up the trail for Sublett's Cutoff. It didn't take long to realize that no matter how much water we carried, it wasn't going to be enough. With so few men left and only a couple of wranglers, it took some doing to keep all the wagons moving. Some would get bogged down in the ruts and need lots of help to get going again. It was probably because of all the weight of the barrels filled with water. Even those were running low.

Then an axel had to be replaced. That took some time. It was the same wagon that had broken down a few times before. Wondered if they'd be able to keep up. We couldn't leave them, of course. We were in unknown Indian country and what with our government relocating so many of the tribes; it was hard to tell who was friendly and who wanted our scalps. Not sure if that was the right solution - taking their land and all and pushing them out. We often saw them in the distance but would ignore them except for keeping an extra watch at night. We kept our cattle and livestock inside when we circled the wagons at night and hoped for the best.

Brian was the oldest of what could be called the boys and he, along with Jacob, did more than his share of assisting up and down the line.

"Someone needs to go ahead to see if we can find water," said Mr. Applegate. Odd how he'd lost his rosy cheeks and ready smile. There were new furrows between his brow and his mouth was most times in a grim line.

"We could send out the three men to scout and bring back water," said Miz Applegate. She was so changed from just a few months on the trail. Had I changed that much too? No matter, there were decisions to talk about.

"Rafferty and the other wrangler can stay back to protect the train. The boys and some of the girls are all pretty decent shots," added Mr. Barnes, looking right at me. "Indians in this neck of the woods aren't supposed to be too evil." He looked down at the hard dried earth that he was poking at with the toe of his boot. "Might just take a couple of days," he said.

Seemed most of us were pretty tired out and didn't have a lot to say. Somehow it was decided. Don't remember exactly who said what but the next morning the three trotted off in different directions. Their horses were looking like it wasn't going to be any too soon to get to water and grass.

"I'm thinking," said Jacob as I was reaching down to collect more of the buffalo chips. "Maybe you girls should change into long pants."

"Why don't you just hop down from that horse and help me pick up some of these chips and stop being so bossy," was my answer. Every now and again, I would pick one up that was still damp underneath. The smell wasn't any too pleasant. The words that came to mind when I would get this stinky mess on my fingers could not be expressed. But we needed every bit and it had to be done, it was the only fuel we had for our cook fires.

We were lucky to have it - Never heard of such back in Virginia. Back there we had seasoned wood from the nearby forests. Out here there didn't seem to be too many trees so we picked up what the buffalo left behind. It burned well enough but it sure could stink if the pile hadn't aged a bit.

But I wondered, why wasn't he down here picking up this stuff with us. He read my mind. "Maddie, you're not the only one that's working you know." He really could be exasperating sometimes.

"Whyn't you more like Randy? Why do you always have to be so bossy and always be right?" I swiped at the beads of sweat dripping off my face. Randy was long gone and I didn't need to keep bringing him up. Jacob missed him as much as I did.

He looked down at me from high up on his horse, like I was some kind of vermin. "There are some things you just don't know," he said and pulled on the reins and trotted away.

What was he saying? There was no time to worry about it. Between Gabriella and Abigail Cantrell and even Jane Applegate, we decided to wear long pants. Maybe Jacob was right. Maybe it wouldn't be so easy for anyone to tell that it was a wagon train filled with mostly women and children. Now in the heat and with no grazing grass and very little water left, we traveled until near pitch dark. It cooled some as the sun went down.

Jane Applegate was the one to discover her father's body.

Guess the rest of us should've seen it first but we didn't. There he was all bloated up from the heat, lying on his back a few yards off the trail.

She had been walking alongside her wagon when she spotted him lying there. It was hard not to recognize the faded red shirt he always wore. Don't know how she kept herself so together. Her brothers and mother certainly didn't.

We stopped long enough to bury him. Couldn't do it that night so waited 'til the light of the new day peaked over the horizon.

By noon the sun was near scorching us. We girls in men's pants had taken to wearing the boy's hats too to keep some of the sun off. Rafferty

Jones actually offered me his, but I think I'd rather have my brains fried in the sun than accept anything from that man. It wasn't his one eye or anything; it was just a look about him or a coldness. Even Hannah felt it and would hide whenever he came around.

"So," said Jacob, "he offered his other hat to you, what's up with saying no?"

Why would he even ask me that? But his eyes were boring into me like my answer was very important or something. I ignored him and put on one of the Uncle's hats that I had found in the trunk.

It was a full two days before we found Mr. Runyon. He was lying next to a small pool of water with a white scum on the top, looked like he hadn't been dead too long. He was with the two horses, both dead, but Mr. Barnes wasn't with him.

It was the water. We had to whip the oxen and the livestock to get them past that oversized puddle. There had been a warning sign that some other travelers had put up but it was in the dirt and we didn't see it 'til we were past the hole. It said "POSEN. Do not drink."

"We have to stop," wailed Mrs. Barnes. "We can't leave him here." She didn't ask or even mention where Mr. Barnes was. Guess seeing his dead horse was enough.

The grief, the wailing, was I ever going to get used to it? In the end, some of the boys wrapped him in a sheet and put him in one of the supply wagons. We'd bury him further down the trail. It wasn't worth the risk to stay there and have the other animals drinking the poisoned water.

"Comes from the alkali in the soil," was Rafferty's contribution. He sure was keeping himself scarce. Not a bad thing, I decided.

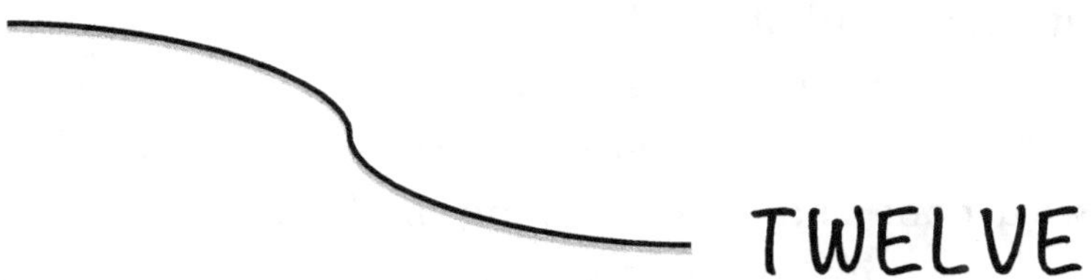

TWELVE

We had just crossed the Snake River when Miz Runyon decided to have that baby. The water was low so we'd been lucky when we crossed at some of the shallow places. Guess they called it the Snake cause it snaked along so much we had to cross it three times to stay on the trail. But it was water so we didn't want to complain.

Don't know why Miz Runyon took this time to have that baby. Maybe it was the fright or maybe the constant rocking or maybe it was the realization that she didn't have a husband anymore. But I don't think so, the husband part that is. By my way of thinking, she was fortunate to be shed of that man.

No matter what the reason, that baby was going to be early. Miz Victoria, her spinster sister who went through most days tight-lipped and disapproving, looked as though she were about to become unglued. She was wringing her hands and pacing back and forth. Guess her specialty was dead bodies not live babies. She'd helped lay out just about all of our dead so far.

Miz Applegate and Miz Barnes went to be with her. We'd circled up for the night right after we'd done that last crossing of the Snake River. There's only so much yelling a body can listen to while we bounced along in the wagons, 'til we all decided it was time to pull over. All the bouncing was good for turning milk into butter but didn't help much when there was a baby wanting to come out. Besides we were all women 'cepting Brian and my brother Jacob, seems they were the closest to being the two oldest. A couple of wranglers were still with us but they kept to themselves. Well, we decided we were going to stop for the night and that was that. Guess those boys had never heard a woman birthing a baby and they lit out, said they needed to get some fresh meat for dinner.

Abigail and Gabriella and I took our wash down to be scrubbed in the river, might as well take advantage of the freshwater and remaining daylight. While we were there we decided to take a cake of soap and wash our hair. It'd been so long. We had taken off our shirts and our camisoles. They were brown with trail dust. Scrub as we might we couldn't get out most of that grime so we waded in and started to work on our hair.

Jane Applegate joined us. She'd changed some. Not sure if now it was a hopeless look she walked around with or one of just accepting what was to be, but she saw us romping and splashing around in the water and within a minute she had her shirt and boots off too. We played and splashed and swam 'til we looked like a bunch of wrinkled white prunes. It felt so good.

"Think she'll make it?" asked Abigail.

"Who?" I asked

"Well and who do you think?" asked Jane.

"Not so sure," answered Gabriella. "I've seen my share of babies born down with the Mexicans who lived on our ranch and most that yelled that much didn't make it."

We were all quiet for a while. Miz Runyon had had more than her share of bad luck what with losing her spinster sister and then losing her husband to poison water. Losing him may not have been such a bad thing, him being such a hot head and all.

Guess I shouldn't think that way. Miz Runyon was pretty enough in a kind of severe way and shouldn't have much trouble finding someone else once we got ourselves settled, I guess if she made it.

But for now, we were here. The women on the train wouldn't let us set off again 'til she was settled with that baby no matter the outcome. And as if to let us know that things weren't going so well a scream drifted down to where we were. The four of us knew our day of play was over as we waded to the shore.

Jane must have seen them first; she elbowed me in the waist. Why hadn't we been paying attention, what had we been thinking, especially with the boys gone off hunting?

There at the river's edge standing between our clothes and us were a dozen or so Indians, their eyes glued on us. My heart was in my throat. There was no way to get up to the wagons to our rifles. How could we have been so careless? The four of us froze in the water.

They had to be Shoshone that was the tribe around this area. They all looked like they were dressed for a party, the women in deerskin skirts with pieces of fur hanging down on the edges. Their tops were decorated with colored beads and they had leather thongs woven in their braids. The men had rows and rows of bone necklaces hanging from their necks to their waists.

We tried to cover ourselves as they stared at us and then goodness me – they were smiling at us. The women put their hands over their mouths trying not to laugh. We all had our boy britches on and we were stark naked on the top. Guess they couldn't figure what we were boy or girl or both. With the smiles, we knew we'd be all right and with the entire group ogling us, we came up on shore and dressed pulling our hair up again under our hats. No one spoke, but they sure could stare at a body. We picked up our clean laundry and headed back up to the wagons. They followed close behind, leaving their horses to graze by the river.

"Who are they?" asked April.

"They've gotta be the Shoshone," I answered. "They're supposed to be friendly, sometimes — just don't rile them. They have their women with them so chances are they're not going to make too much trouble." With this Miz Runyon let out a piercing scream that sent shivers up my spine.

One of the Indian women, looking older than the others, with her face covered with a red dye, looked at me as if to ask what are we doing to that poor woman. I pointed to my belly and then pretended to rock a baby and she nodded and said "Ahhh."

Her hands flew up as she made hand signs and spoke a language that I had no way of following. She was talking with her hands as fast as she was talking with her mouth. She pointed to the sky and then the sun and made a sign as if the sun were setting.

"She means how long has she been this way?" said Jane. I held up two fingers figuring that must mean two days. Again she said "Ahhh." This seemed to be the only word that I could grasp. Then she came over and took my arm and pushed me towards the Runyon's wagon.

'Course Miz Victoria was pacing outside back and forth, her hands about wrung out when she looked up and saw that old Indian woman coming at her. You'd have thought she'd seen a ghost. She turned, hiked up her stiff black bombazine dress, let out a screech and ran. The Indian woman ignored her and continued pushing and dragging me towards the wagon. I brought her to the rear where she stuck her head in.

"We have company," I said to Miz Barnes and Miz Applegate, figuring I didn't want them heading for the hills too. They looked up from their work, nodded and then went back to sponging Miz Runyon's face.

"She sure doesn't look good does she," I said, knowing full well the old woman couldn't understand a word I said.

Miz Barnes heard me and said real low, "I'm

afraid if it's not born soon, it's going to kill her."

The Indian held up a finger and made some motions with her hands.

Jane had appeared by my side and said, "I think she's telling you she's going away somewhere but will be back." I nodded my head as though I understood her and then looked at Jane wondering how she knew all this.

The old Indian smiled at me, the red dye making her wrinkles look even deeper. She squeezed my arm and then did a pigeon-toed run walk, the fringe of her skirt slapping against her legs. She went back to where they all had first appeared. The rest of the tribe was busy peeking into the wagons and poking at different things as if they'd never seen the like. You could tell they were uncomfortable with all the screaming going on. They wandered back to the river where they had left their horses.

"Here they come again," announced Abigail our self-appointed sentry. We decided we were much too lax without having someone as the lookout, and we had been really remiss in leaving the circle of wagons without a gun. We decided that would not happen again.

My Indian friend, her moccasins swishing across the dirt, came up to me. It looked like she'd freshened up the red dye on her face She pulled out a well-worn leather sack held together tightly with a greasy thong. Once again she took my arm and pushed and guided me towards Miz Runyon's wagon. It'd been a while and those screams weren't quite so loud or long.

"She wants to go in," said Jane, translating the hand language before I could ask. Together we climbed up through the back of the wagon. She made more hand language as well as speaking softly in her own tongue and then as if by magic Jane appeared with a cup of water.

The woman shook some of the gray powder into the cup and stirred it up with her finger, it was none too clean, but maybe that was supposed to be part of the mixture. She handed it to Miz Applegate, but she shook her head no.

"I don't want that," she said. The Indian pointed to Miz Runyon and Jane said, "It's to make the baby come." The two women waved her away.

"No mother," said Jane. "She wants Miz Runyon to drink it to help her along." Miz Applegate looked at her daughter. It'd be my guess that was the first time she'd ever spoken up to her mother. Lo and behold, maybe just because she was in such shock that her daughter would speak that way, she took the cup and held it to Miz Runyon's lips. Now getting her to drink it was another story entirely but with some coaxing and getting the Indian out of the wagon, the two women got her to drink most of it.

Jane and I brought the old woman over to our fire and got her to sit. I gave her some corn bread with lots of butter slathered on it and watched as she gobbled it up. It was nice to find someone who wasn't sick to death of cornbread. Then she took a stick and started to draw a picture in the dirt as she pointed to the bag.

"It's a rattlesnake," said Jane.

"Well, I can certainly see what it is. You don't suppose she's trying to tell us that gray powder came from the rattles of rattlesnake do you?"

"I don't think there's much doubt," said Jane. I guess it would've taken an idiot not to see what she was drawing. My heart was in my throat, what if we'd let this woman poison Miz Runyon? And as if to calm my fears there was a sudden cry from the wagon.

The cry was not from a woman, but from a newborn baby. It was hard to miss. The old Indian smiled so hard her eyes disappeared in her leathery cheeks. She had big white teeth and fine black eyebrows and some sort of animal teeth hanging from her ears. She was about as pleased with herself as she could be. She rocked back and forth and sang a low humming sort of song, keeping the rhythm with her rocking. After a time she rose up and half bowing to us and again using her hand language, departed.

"She said, the big or great spirit is with you."

"How do you know all this," I asked Jane. I guess the surprise must have shown in my face.

"I watch people." Guess that was the answer, anyway the only answer she was going to give me.

We were sorry to see the old Indian woman leave. I was sorry we couldn't speak her language. We went over and peeked in the wagon and there was the tiniest baby I'd ever seen. Miz Barnes said it was a girl and she shook her head as if to say no. She didn't need words to tell us more.

Later, after our dinner was cleared away, we sat to enjoy the open sky filled with stars. Miz Applegate came to join us. "The babe won't make it," she said. "She's much too small."

"I guess babies don't do very well on the trail," I said for lack of anything better. Gabriella looked at me as though she took that personally. Baby Sara was of course in her lap, still struggling to make it through each day. Our milk cow was not doing very well. I wasn't sure how much longer we'd be getting anything from her.

Gabriella was very attached to that baby, with her mother dead and all, she'd practically made it her own. If anything happened to that little thing, I feared for her. She wouldn't take it easily, seemed that all her love and affection and attention went into that little bundle. She pulled little Sara closer and got up and left. Guess I shouldn't have spoken out.

~

It wasn't more than a couple of days later that all hell broke loose. There we were feeling calmed and safe and not worrying much about thunderstorms, or fires or even Indians when Jacob came in to announce, "He's gone."

"Who's gone," I asked, there weren't all that many "he's" who were still left. My mind did a quick calculation: "You mean Brian?" I asked. My heart skipped a beat for whatever reason.

"No, Rafferty." His jaw was tight, he had a look like Father did when he was about to explode.

"What do you mean?"

"I mean he's gone. Rafferty's gone. So are the horses."

"How could they be? Those Indians wouldn't steal our horses."

"Wasn't the Indians," he said.

My mouth must have fallen open and words failed me. Hannah, with her usual silence, hid behind me.

"Don't think he's coming back either." He took a moment as though chewing things over thinking about what to say next. "Money's gone too."

"No, it's not," I said, "It's down in the cornmeal barrel in the wooden box."

"No, it isn't Madison." He was using his mature voice on me.

"Why do you always know everything?" I was getting really angry. "I wish Randy was here," I said. "Not you." And there, I did it again. I do not know when to hold my tongue.

"He's dead," said Jacob. "Just like everyone else."

I did not want to hear him. I stomped over to the barrel. I dug in that cornmeal up to my armpits. The box was not there. I turned to look at him.

"When are you going to smarten up?" he asked.

"What are you talking about?"

"Don't you know anything?" His anger at me

and at everything had nearly brought tears to his eyes.

"What exactly am I supposed to know?"

"Madison didn't Uncle David tell you."

"Tell me what for heaven's sake? You mean about Isabelle?" Maybe I should've said *Aunt* Isabelle, but I thought I'll work on that one later.

"No, about Rafferty and Randy. I thought he told you."

"He said their names, that's all."

"Well," he said, "It's time you knew." He took a deep breath, "Your long-deceased brother Randy was a thief and a liar. The brother you idolized so much was in with Rafferty on his scheme. They were together in the horse thievery back on the farm."

I thought I heard a sob in his voice as he spoke. I had no words so it wasn't hard, for once, to keep still. Jacob had a rock in his hand and he kept slamming it from one hand to the next like he was trying to crush something.

So what was I to say? Odd when I need my words they fail me.

"Maddie," he said a bit more kindly, "I think Rafferty shot and killed Randy. Father never knew, or he wasn't sure." There was a great sigh. At least he wasn't still trying to crush that fool rock with his bare hands.

"The Uncles suspected. They didn't want Rafferty on this wagon train, but didn't know how to get rid of him. Sadie's mother told them just before we left. She said she'd heard them talking down by the slave's quarters. She said they'd been arguing. She said it sounded like Randy had taken up with Rafferty in his horse thieving just to see if he could get away with it. Sadie's mom said it sounded like he wanted out. Randy was involved only a couple of times and he didn't want to be part of it anymore. She said she heard a gunshot soon after that and the next day they found Randy." He didn't take a breath during this entire speech.

He gave that rock one final crushing slam then heaved it as hard as he could outside the circle of wagons.

What he said could not have been true. My big brother, the boy that practically raised me? "Did Father know?" I think it was a whisper and I'm not sure I wanted an answer.

"He may have suspected, but do you think he would've allowed Rafferty to come with us if he knew he'd killed his son."

"Did Isabelle know?"

"No one *knew* anything. It was all hearsay. I

don't know how we could ever prove it. Course there's Hannah but she's not speaking."

"What does she have to do with it?"

"Maddie, didn't you notice when she stopped talking?"

"I guess, but I thought she was so upset that Randy was dead that she just stopped speaking."

"Well there may be more to it, but I don't know yet."

Somehow I couldn't absorb this. It wasn't true. I just knew it. Jacob was jealous of Randy I was sure of it. Randy had been my favorite brother. He'd been so much fun. We always had such a good time together. Jacob was always the good one. He did his chores. He never argued and he was always where he was supposed to be. That had to be it, Jacob was still jealous of Randy.

"We're going to have to push on," he said to my silence. "We need to get moving or we're going to be meeting up with winter and if you think it's been tough going so far, wait'll you see a wagon in snow."

"How do you know so much?" I asked.

"I listen," he said.

THIRTEEN

We left in the morning. The sun was hardly up. Brian had dug the hole for the Runyon baby – alone. It wasn't a very big hole. We stood and watched as Miz Victoria lowered the tiny bundle into the hole. The tiny bundle was wrapped tightly in a patchwork quilt of bright yellows and reds. It was the one Miz Runyon had been working on for most of the trip. It didn't fit the occasion I thought, but then we were running out of flannel sheets to bury our dead. Odd how things worked out; the unnamed babe had waited 'til we crossed into Oregon Country to make her appearance and then to lose her so quickly.

This day wasn't quite so long as some of the others. The trail was well marked with the ruts of the wagons that had gone before us. Our small band circled up well before the sun went down. We had time to collect the buffalo chips and a few pieces of wood for the fire. We were having the last of the bacon for dinner with beans. Maybe when we got off the trail, if life was good to me, I'd never again have to see another bean.

The campsite had just about settled for the night when our Indian friends rode back in. We knew they had been following us but it wasn't a problem. Maybe they were watching out for us. This time though there were only six of them, which included our healer. She smiled her funny smile as her eyes again disappeared into her reddened cheeks. And then as quickly as she had smiled, her face fell as she turned and looked back. Following a few paces behind was a young Indian man leading a horse. He had a few raggedy feathers stuck in his braids that were tied together with rawhide. His face looked to me like it had a permanent scowl.

He hadn't been part of the group that stood by the river a couple of days ago when they laughed at us in our half-naked attire. His chest was bare and he had only one necklace draped around his neck. It was a string of what looked like bear's teeth. We stood and watched as he led the horse in. I knew that horse. I knew him as well as I knew my one remaining ox. The ox that I had been driving every day since April.

The horse that he was leading in was one of father's horses.

It didn't take much to figure who the body was lying across his back. The body didn't have his hat on and his hair was hanging down in dirty black strings.

~

The night was quiet. Brian and Jacob had thrown their shovels aside and were brushing down the horses. I noticed that the grave they just dug wasn't piled very high with rocks. The rocks were to keep the wolves from digging up the burial site.

The old Indian woman sat at our fire enjoying yet more of the cornbread, this time with no butter. Old Betsy had about given out in the milk department. What little I was getting out of her was now all going to Gabriella in her attempt to keep Sara alive. And there she was, standing by my campfire holding the tiny bundle coming to see if there was any milk left. The Indian woman watched in silence as Gabriella tried to get the baby to take more than a few teaspoons of the warmish milk. It was so thin it was bluish.

The Indian watched. She shook her head no and held out her arms for the little one. Gabriella seemed reluctant but passed the small bundle to the waiting arms. Speaking softly in her singsong voice she smiled and cooed and murmured to the child. When she rose up, cradling her against her deerskin robe, Gabriella came to attention. She stood very close to the Indian, fearing maybe that she was going to walk off with the baby. Cradling her and speaking in a whisper, the old Indian walked over to Miz Runyon's wagon. We could hear small weeping sounds coming from the inside. The distraught mother was not going to get over her loss easily.

Hoisting herself up over the back of the wagon, the Indian woman disappeared inside with tiny Sara in her arms.

The quiet sobs coming from the wagon were muffled and then stopped. Moments later the wagon creaked as the Indian woman emerged. She hopped down, this time without baby Sara. A smile that again hid her eyes behind her leathery cheeks showed her pleasure. She nodded in satisfaction and taking us both by the arm, led us back to the fire.

All was quiet. We sat awhile and poked at the embers. We spoke in low voices as if we somehow would disturb the peace of the evening if we spoke too loud.

"Is he dead?" said a voice.

It came out of the darkness. I didn't think I

heard what I thought I heard and ignored it. I poked at the fire hoping to get it to share a bit of its warmth. Trying to keep the small flames from dying out I continued poking at it. We were so comfortable watching as the stars began to show themselves, one by one in the night sky. I was sure I could pick out the Big Dipper and the Little Dipper and I was sure I'd seen a shooting star.

"Is he dead?" There it was again. I turned. Standing behind me was Hannah, her young and trusting eyes looking at me, pleading almost.

"Is who dead?" I asked, for a moment not realizing who I was speaking to. "Hannah," I nearly shouted. "Hannah," I said again. I jumped up and caught myself as I started to fall from tripping on the log. I scooped her up. "Is who dead sweetheart?" I looked at her, this beautiful child who had been locked in her silence for so long.

"That man Rafferty." Her voice sounded a bit raspy but was so good to hear.

"Yes, he's dead," I said. "We don't know how but it was him alright. That's who Jacob and Brian just buried." Was I really talking to this silent child?

She let a great sigh escape. I must have shown some surprise at this as she snuck her arms up around me and hugged me.

"He was bad." She said. Her voice was muffled

against my neck.

I'm sure I gasped but didn't want to frighten her back into her silence.

"Would you like to tell me why?" My voice I hoped was calm and quiet.

"He killed Randy."

Then I did gasp. I sat back down and wrapped my arms around her. She snuggled into my lap.

The night wore on; we had added more wood to what was now a cheery fire. By the time I had the whole story, the old Indian woman was fast asleep in her blanket, her feet close to the warmth of the flames. Jacob and Gabriella and I sat without speaking. Hannah had talked herself out and was curled up, asleep. The sound of her quiet breathing was comforting.

"She's been frightened for almost two years," said Jacob. "Ever since he killed Randy."

"So Sadie's mother was right. Rafferty did kill him. I'm just sorry Hannah had to see it."

"He threatened her if she talked." Jacob shook his head in disbelief.

"Guess it was the only way to keep her from telling. But to tell a little girl you'll cut her tongue out if she so much as whispers a word..."

"Guess he got his," said Jacob. "'Pears it was an arrow that got him but not from the Shoshone.

Maybe the Cayuse, that's who he was trying to sell the horses to."

"Will we get any of them back?" I asked.

"Unlikely but his saddlebag was filled with money, I guess most of it came from the sale of the horses that he stole back home."

"Didn't Father know?" I asked.

Jacob said no. He said he probably suspected but sometimes we don't want to know the truth, even hide from it - even adults he said. Randy was his first-born son. How could anyone believe that of their child? That he'd been part of horse thievin'.

Odd how Father had wanted to move on to Oregon Country so soon after Randy was shot. More than likely, he probably had an idea about it, but just didn't want to find out.

We sat by the fire until late into the night. The moon was settling itself behind the mountain range far off in the distance; it lit up the night with a warm glow. It couldn't be far now, I thought, maybe just a couple of week's worth of travel.

In the morning we left. It was later than usual, taking our time breaking camp and saying goodbye to the Shoshone, our new friends. From there, it wasn't far to reach the Barlow Road. It was new and it was a toll road and they said it would cut off what would be a treacherous journey down the

Columbia River. The uncles had told us we'd try to travel some other way because traveling down that river could be a very dangerous route. And here we were. Not sure if the Uncles even knew of this new road.

The toll was all right; we had all that money from dead Rafferty. He had no family and no doubt it all was accumulated from the sale of our stolen horses.

There was a letter waiting for us as we paid to get through. The toll man who took our money said they were often pressed into service to act as a postal delivery system as it was quickly becoming a very popular cut through. 'Course the letter had been there for a couple of months addressed to Uncle Bert and Uncle David.

It was from Father. He said he was waiting for us. He was in the Willamette Valley and if we'd made it this far safely, there wouldn't be too many more obstacles. Not the easiest road he said as it had just opened, but lots easier than any other way.

We devoured the letter, hanging on every word as Jacob read it to us. Father wrote that if it was too difficult, we should get word to him and he'd come and travel with us for the last part of the trail. He sounded excited with the farm he'd created. He said he already had two dozen horses. He also said he knew we were all safe with Uncle David and Uncle Bert leading us. He said he could not wait to see everyone and hoped Isabelle was doing better. Oh, I thought if he only knew. So much had happened.

Gabriella and I sat on the wagon bench with Hannah between us. It wouldn't be much further now. The road was clear. There'd be challenges for these last few days or maybe even weeks, but it would be hard to imagine that it could be any worse than what we'd been through.

We would meet up with Father soon enough and then we could begin our new life. A life without so many upheavals. Maybe a life with some peace. A life with a sister who could speak again. A life that could include my new friend, Gabriella, and maybe Brian for a neighbor and maybe even Jane and Abigail would consider settling in the new valley near us.

It wouldn't be much further. We had made it to Oregon Country.

THE END

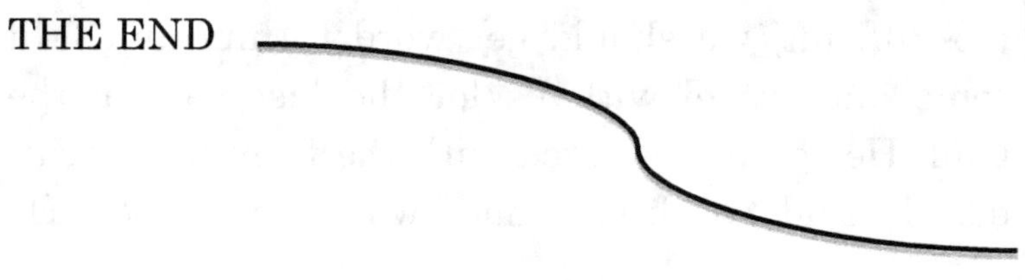

BIBLIOGRAPHY

Bodett, T. (1997). *America's Historic Trails.* San Francisco: KQED Books.

Bowen, William A. (1978). *The Willamette Valley: Migration and Settlement on the Oregon Frontier.* Seattle: Univ. of Washington Press.

Dickson, A., Editor. (1989).*Covered Wagon Days From the Private Journals of Albert Jerome Dickson.* Lincoln: University of Nebraska Press.

Hubalek, L. (1995). *Trail of Thread.* Lindsborg: Butterfield Books Inc.

Lewis, Jon E. (2001). *The West.* New York: Carroll & Graf Publishers.

Peavey L. (1996). *Pioneer Women.* Norman: University of Oklahoma Press.

Stewart G. (1962). *The California Trail.* New York: First McGraw-Hill.

FACTOIDS

1. In 1805, two years after the Louisiana Purchase, Lewis & Clark, under the direction of President Thomas Jefferson, set out from St. Louis, Missouri for the west. Their goal was to establish a presence in the unknown Northwest Territory as well as to explore and map a way to the Pacific Ocean.

2. Lewis and Clarke met up with mountain men and fur trappers who were already busy in the west with a thriving trade in beaver pelts. Beaver was a valuable fur that was shipped east and to Europe for hats and clothing.

3. Missionaries began arriving in Oregon Country in the early 1830s. Their goal was to bring Christianity to the American Indians. England signed over their rights to the Oregon Country in 1846, allowing the U.S. to claim the land below the 49th parallel. Oregon became a state in 1859.

4. In 1836 the first wagon trains set out for the unknown lands to the west. It is estimated that of the 400,000 Oregon Trail emigrants only 80,000 ended their journey in Oregon's Willamette Valley. Many of the settlers splintered off from the wagon trains to settle in Wyoming or Idaho. Others took the cutoff to California.

5. In 1848 gold was discovered in California. An estimated 90,000 of the 49ers (named for the year they set out) headed out west in hopes of striking it rich.

6. Many of the pioneers died along the trail from accidents such as drowning, or gunshot or disease. There were also fires, unpredictable weather and an unreliable food supply for the animals.

7. With ideal conditions, the wagon trains could travel 10 - 20 miles per day. However ideal conditions were rare as they dealt with weather, accidents, river crossings and breakdowns.

8. Not all trails were well known or well marked. The pioneers often blazed their own trails, which sometimes led them into dangerous territories where there was a lack of good grazing land for cattle or lack of water or unfriendly Indians. Wheel ruts from the more well-traveled trails can still be seen today in states such as Nebraska and Wyoming.

9. Each wagon needed to provision for the trip as there were few trading posts along the way. For a family of four that would include 400 pounds of flour, 75 pounds of bacon, five pounds of coffee, ten pounds of rice, as well as sugar, dried beans, salt, cornmeal and any medicines that they may need along the trail such as turpentine, oil of peppermint, laudanum and castor oil.

10. In 1869 the transcontinental railway was completed. This connected the east coast to the west coast, thus shortening the often hazardous and months long trip to a few days.

Antietam
Waking the Fury

Emily at 15 is bored and annoyed with just about everything and everybody. Tired of her chores and irritated by the endless care of three younger sisters, she would like to have a life of her own. Her parents are absent; her Father is off fighting a war she doesn't understand and her Mother has left for Pennsylvania. As the eldest of the four sisters, she must take responsibility for her home and family. When the bloodiest battle of the Civil War is fought almost on her doorstep she is unwillingly pressed into service. Emily is called on to make decisions and to take charge of wounded soldiers while fending off the invading troops and protecting her younger sisters. Life changes forever as she discovers a courage that she did not know she possessed. Strengths emerge as she stands up for her beliefs while sheltering the enemy and caring for a runaway slave, both of which hold very serious consequences. In this remarkably accurate depiction of the Battle of Antietam, a legend is once more uncovered. It involves a mass of very angry bees. This dangerous, stinging swarm may well have had an influence on the outcome of that fateful day in 1862.

Now available at Amazon, Apple, Nook (Barnes and Noble), Kobo and other online retailers in print and digital editions!

Jennie Wade: A Girl From Gettysburg

It had been foolish to stay but now there was no choice. It was anyone's guess what the outcome would be. Nothing was as it should be. Oddly, the Confederate troops were pouring in from the north and Union troops were marching in from the south. They arrived in droves. The town was not prepared for what happened during the early days of the summer, 1863. Jennie, a young local girl, did her best to keep up with the demand for bread and water and medical care for the troops. Her brothers were scattered, her sister would soon be having a baby, her mother was not bearing up well and Jack, her intended, had not been heard from in weeks. It was a time and place that would be recorded in American history forever. A time marked by the largest number of casualties in the Civil War. It was Gettysburg, Pennsylvania, a small, unremarkable town; an easily forgotten town that would live in infamy and one that history would never forget. Of the almost 50,000 casualties of that encounter in early July, only one civilian was killed. This is her story. The story of Jennie Wade, a dedicated young woman thrown into the middle of one of Americans' most tragic times.

Now available at Amazon, Apple, Nook (Barnes and Noble), Kobo and other online retailers in print and digital editions!

Mists of the Blue Ridge

Olivia lived a quiet and protected life tucked away on a farm in the Blue Ridge Mountains. It was far from the great war that had been raging between the North and the South. She had little interest in the who and the why of it all, and wasn't even sure where her sympathies lay. Then, without warning, the conflict surrounded her. At 16, she was ill prepared for the responsibilities that were thrust on her.

This is her story. It's a tale that tells of courage, determination and survival during one of America's most trying times.

Now available at Amazon, Apple, Nook (Barnes and Noble), Kobo and other online retailers in print and digital editions!

Hidden in the Early Light
a tale of the Irish famine

Katy was 16 when the hard times came. Her father disappeared in the night and her mother left her with a tiny baby sister. She was suddenly thrust into the role of caretaker. It was a responsibility she didn't want. The farming life was not for her and now she had to find a way to survive and to keep her younger brothers from starving. How could she ever be free of a life she hadn't chosen?

It was the 1840s and thousands were dying from the great potato famine, one of history's most dreadful events.

This is Katy's story, the story of how a young girl survived by using her wits, determination and courage.

Now available at Amazon, Apple, Nook (Barnes and Noble), Kobo and other online retailers in print and digital editions!

Shadows in the Fog:
A Block Island Tale

Molly lived on an island far away from the mainland. She was an orphan and there was no one to care for her. Sent to live in a house filled with boys she was pressed into the role of cook and caretaker. Her life became that of a servant.

When an unfortunate incident took place that threatened to scar her forever, she was sent to live with an angered and bitter veteran of the Civil War. Living the life of a recluse and with battle scars of his own, he keeps his past hidden from all. Hidden until Molly comes to stay.

This is the tale of a young girl's quest for survival and how she brings herself out of the depths of despair as she learns of her mysterious past. Uplifting and compelling, the tale follows Molly as she matures and accepts all that life has given her.

Now available at Amazon, Apple, Nook (Barnes and Noble), Kobo and other online retailers in print and digital editions!

Gift of the Winds
A Tale of Hendricks Head Lighthouse

In the late 1800s a ferocious nor'easter traveled up the New England coast. It forced a three-masted schooner up on the rocks. It was within sight of the Hendricks Head Lighthouse. History says there were no survivors. However, a trunk was found that had been washed ashore. It held a most unusual and interesting surprise.

The tale unfolds through Abigail's diary. It tells of the unfortunate event that condemned her to the life of a recluse in Ireland. Life is difficult for her, but determined to survive; an inner strength takes over. Alone, she sets out for a new life in America.

Now available at Amazon, Apple, Nook (Barnes and Noble), Kobo and other online retailers in print and digital editions!

Andersonville: The Long Journey Home

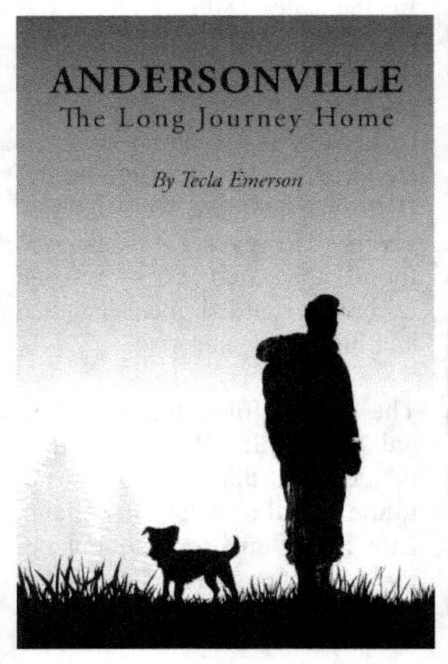

Hock snuck off in the dark of night to join the Union Army. He was too young to be part of the fighting force but now, taller than most, he easily joined their ranks. Wounded in the battle at Petersburg he was captured and sent to a Confederate prisoner-of-war camp – a camp so horrid, it is still written of today. As one more of Andersonville's nameless inmates, he was given a number. Identified as "Unknown 9586," he was thrown on the death cart and hauled out as one of the dead. "Unknown 9586," did not rest in peace. Leaving the site of his burial, he set out for the north. Alone, starving, wounded and unarmed he began his journey. This is his story. From the hills of Vermont to the sights and scenes of horror that are found on battlefields and then to his final destination. It's the tale of prisoner #9586 – Unknown. The prisoner who missed his own burial.

Now available at Amazon, Apple, Nook (Barnes and Noble), Kobo and other online retailers in print and digital editions!

The Letter

"My being for ever banished from your sight..."

Who was this "...undutiful and Disobedient Child" who in 1756 penned a letter to her father in England? What had she done to so offend him? Why, as a well educated young girl, had she become an indentured servant? Why was she alone?

In her letter, she pleads with her father to forgive her and to at least send her a bit of clothing. "...almost naked, no shoes nor stockings to wear." Here, within these pages, the mystery of Elizabeth Sprigs is revealed. It is a tale based on a single letter sent from Baltimore so long ago.

Now available at Amazon, Apple, Nook (Barnes and Noble), Kobo and other online retailers in print and digital editions!